LOST IN THE RIVER OF GRASS

LOST IN THE RIVER OF GRASS

GINNY RORBY

carolrhoda LAB

MINNEAPOLIS

Carolrhoda Lab™
An imprint of Carolrhoda Books
A division of Lerner Publishing Group, Inc.
241 First Avenue North
Minneapolis, MN 55401 U.S.A.

Website address: www.lernerbooks.com

Cover photograph for hard cover edition © Nativestock Pictures/Photolibrary.
Cover photograph for paperback edition © Stephen Frink Collection/Alamy.

Library of Congress Cataloging-in-Publication Data

Rorby, Ginny.
    Lost in the river of grass / by Ginny Rorby.
        p. cm.
    Summary: When two Florida teenagers become stranded on a tiny island in the Everglades, they attempt to walk ten miles through swampland to reach civilization.
    ISBN: 978-0-7613-5685-1
    [1. Wilderness survival—Fiction. 2. Survival—Fiction. 3. Friendship—Fiction.
4. Animals—Florida—Everglades—Fiction. 5. Everglades (Fla.)—Fiction.] I. Title.
PZ7.R69Lo 2011
    [Fic]—dc22   2009053999

Manufactured in the United States of America
4 – SB – 7/1/12

This is dedicated to my husband,
Doug Oesterle,
to whom this story belongs;
to the memory of Bob Kelley,
who defined friendship;
and to Oscar "Bud" Owre,
who taught me to love
the Everglades.
I miss you both.
And to the real Mr. Vickers,
my seventh-grade
science teacher.

"The miracle of the light pours over the green and brown expanse of saw grass and of water, shining and slow-moving below, the grass and water that is the meaning and the central fact of the Everglades of Florida. It is a river of grass."

—Marjorie Stoneman Douglas,
The Everglades: River of Grass

. . .

"the world is mud-luscious...
the world is puddle-wonderful"

—e. e. cummings, "[in Just-]"

. . .

"Those who contemplate the beauty of the earth find reserves of strength that will endure as long as life lasts."

—Rachel Carson, *The Sense of Wonder*

DAY ONE

1

Mr. Vickers takes the seat behind the bus driver. The other fourteen kids pile in behind him in pairs, like ark animals. Since I'm last on the bus, my choice is to sit next to him or sit alone. He's left room for me, but is nice enough not to say anything when I drag my gear to the back row.

The ride to where we're going in the Everglades is long, and a hot, gritty, diesel-smelling wind swirls in through the open windows. I've been staring out at the same scenery for an hour: a long, straight, black water canal, a levee, and miles and miles of saw grass.

My poor parents thought they'd died and gone to heaven when I got accepted into Glades Academy this year, but school started three weeks ago and I hate it more every day. I either feel invisible or like a sore thumb. No one talks *to* me, just about me.

This weekend field trip wasn't required, so it didn't occur to me to sign up. First off, I couldn't care less about seeing a swamp, and secondly, it cost more than my parents could really afford, but Mr. Vickers, my science teacher, talked me into it. "Divide and conquer, Sarah," he said, as if being with fewer students will give me better odds of making a friend. There are ten boys on the trip and four other girls. The boys are okay, but the girls are clumped together like a tar ball on the beach.

Mr. Vickers feels sorry for me. I can tell because, when he turns to point out something he wants us to notice, he includes me and smiles.

I curl up on the back bench, put my head on my duffel bag, and pretend to sleep in spite of the chatter and laughter from the front.

I guess I did doze off, because when Mr. Vickers calls, "Breakfast stop," I jerk awake, sit up, and look out. We're pulling into the parking lot of the Miccosukee Indian restaurant. I don't feel hungry until I smell bacon frying. Then my stomach starts to growl.

We're expected at the restaurant; a single long table is set for us. I'm the last one in and have to take a seat at the end opposite from Mr. Vickers—teacher at one end and me, the token poor-but-promising student, at the other.

There are two waitresses. When one gets to our end of the table, Adam—at least I think that's his name—orders a hamburger.

"Breakfast only," the waitress says. "No burgers 'til eleven-thirty."

"I don't like eggs. How 'bout a grilled cheese sandwich?"

"Only breakfast until eleven-thirty." She pops her gum.

Two of the girls are named Amanda; the third and fourth are Brittany and Courtney. The Amanda on my right orders a cheese omelet.

"Okay," Adam says. "I'll have a cheese omelet, too, but hold the eggs. Just bring me the cheese, two pieces of wheat toast, and an order of fries."

Brittany, who's sitting next to Adam, giggles.

"Hash browns," the waitress says.

Adam rolls his eyes. "Whatever."

I only have ten dollars with me and can't remember if breakfast is included in the price of the field trip. "I'm not very hungry," I say, and see Mr. Vickers glance up.

"This is all one check," he tells the waitress at his end of the table.

"Come on, dearie." Our waitress drums the pad with her pencil.

I don't look at her. "Two eggs over easy . . ."

"I can't hear you," she says.

"Crisp bacon, pumpkin bread . . ." My stomach growls so loudly, Amanda laughs out loud. "And hash browns, too, please."

Where I live in Coconut Grove there are frequent gunshots, so when an engine backfires in the canal behind the restaurant, I instinctively duck my head and squeeze my eyes shut.

There's another backfire before the engine sputters to life. A moment later, an airboat skims past the rear wall of windows, its benches loaded with tourists. An Indian guide is perched on the seat mounted in front of the cage that covers what was once an airplane's propeller.

"I'd love to ride in one of those," Adam says.

"Me, too," Amanda says.

I don't say anything until Mom's advice pops into my head. *Be friendly. Don't expect them to come to you; you have to make the first move.* "Me, too," I say.

"You, too, what?" Amanda says.

"It would be fun to go for an airboat ride."

"We just said that."

"I know. I'm just agreeing that it would be fun."

She looks at me like I'm the underbelly of an earthworm, then says to Adam, "I've got my mother's Visa, maybe we could talk Mr. Vickers into letting us pay extra and go for a ride. Then again," she stares at me, "probably not, if we couldn't *all* afford to go."

My mother's one of the cooks in the school cafeteria, and I'm on a scholarship—not because she works there. I'm on the swimming team. I'd like to jump in that black water canal and swim out of here. Or better yet, drown Amanda in it, then swim home.

When breakfast comes, my eggs are overcooked and crusty brown on both sides. The bacon's nearly raw, and the hash browns are the shredded frozen kind I hate and still cold in the middle. I eat the center out of one egg, a crispy edge of a strip of bacon, and the pumpkin bread, which is greasy but good.

. . .

The restaurant is almost directly across the highway from the entrance to Everglades National Park. In spite of the forty-five-mile-an-hour speed limit, traffic whizzes by at sixty and seventy. Mr. Vickers makes us all get back on the bus for the ride across the road.

"We're going to take a tram ride out to the observation tower," he shouts when we get there, over the racket of everyone gathering their stuff. "Our driver will stay here, so you can leave your gear. If you have a camera, bring it."

I have an old maroon Wilderness Experience backpack with two separate zippered compartments. I put Dad's camera in the bottom of the pack, my wallet in the top, and follow the others off the bus.

Before the tram ride we have to listen to a park ranger's canned speech about the damage the sugar industry is causing and how endangered the Everglades ecosystem is. I'm listening to his monotone and fanning away mosquitoes as I watch shiny black birds inspect car grills for freshly squashed insects. Out of the corner of my eye, I see a flash of yellow, then hear a thud. I back away from the others and peek around the corner of the park's office building. Lying on the ground beneath a window is the prettiest little bird I've ever seen outside of a pet store. It's bright yellow, with a black bandit mask over its eyes. The window, which reflects the trees like a mirror, shows a dusty print and a few yellow feathers where the bird struck it. I walk over to look more closely. Its sides are still moving. I carefully pick it up and carry it back in cupped hands.

"This poor little bird hit the window," I say to the ranger. "But it's still alive."

Everyone crowds in for a look.

"That's a male Common Yellowthroat warbler," he says. "Best to put it back where you found it. Few survive an impact with a window, so it will die, or come to and fly away."

I don't like this guy. "Something might get it before it has a chance to wake up."

His smile is condescending. "Always best to let nature take its course."

"If the building wasn't there, the bird wouldn't have hit it." I feel my cheeks heat up. I'm not good at speaking my mind. What I want to say is that the building is in the way of nature taking its course. As usual, it hasn't come out right. I walk around the corner, like I'm going to put the bird back under the window, but instead I slide him into the pocket of my dad's shirt, which is tied around my waist.

2

The open-sided tram does a fifteen-mile loop to a concrete observation tower. I slouch in the seat behind the others, put my knees on the bench in front of me, and stare at the flat expanse of saw grass with my right hand cupped over the bird in my pocket. His warm body feels as soft as a wad of cotton against my palm.

The road is just inches above the water level, and the tram moves slowly as Mr. Vickers points out the different birds we pass, turtles sunning on logs, and a couple of alligators.

"What kind is that?" someone shouts and points at a tall white bird with a black, bald head.

Mr. Vickers puts a finger to his lips. "That's a wood stork—North America's only stork."

The tram stops, and the stork lifts its crinkle-skinned head to stare at us. It has black legs and Pepto-Bismol–colored feet. It had been walking slowly and shaking its pink feet beneath the surface before we interrupted it, but it quickly loses interest in us and returns to sweeping its bill back and forth like a blind person's cane through the water.

The bird in my pocket moves slightly. He's waking up. I smile to myself.

I promised Dad to take lots of pictures, and the stork is really close. I unzip the bottom of my backpack quietly, so as not to disturb the bird in my pocket or the stork, and take out his camera—a 1952 Leica IIIf Red Dial range-finder he bought on eBay for a week's salary. He treasures this camera, and when he said he wanted me to take it on the trip, I almost cried.

"I'll be really careful with it, Dad. I promise."

"I'm not worried about it. This baby's the toughest camera in the world, and who knows, maybe this will launch your career as a *National Geographic* photographer."

Dad and I spent last evening together, with him showing me how put film in and take it out, blow dust off the lens, use a special, soft cloth to clean off any fingerprints, and how to focus the image. When I look through the lens, there are two wood storks. To get a sharp picture I have to turn the focus ring until the two images become one. He had me practice so that I'd know how to focus quickly. I bring the two images of the wood stork together, take its picture, then wind the film to be ready for the next shot. The other kids have cameras that click and beep and chirp, but the Leica is almost completely silent.

"They don't hunt what they see like herons and egrets," Mr. Vickers is saying about the stork. "They catch what they feel as they run their bills through shallow water. That means they need a high concentration of fish in a confined area. When the Everglades was a natural system, the winter dry-down left shallow pools full of fish."

The stork shakes to fluff its feathers and pulls out a loose one, which seesaws in the air as it drifts down to float on the water.

"Remember that wall of dirt and shells on the far side of the canal as we drove out? Those are levees built to hold the water inside so-called conservation areas. And all the pumping stations we passed. Those are there to supply our water needs. The storks usually nest in March when the water is low, so there is plenty of food for their young."

The bird shifts in my pocket. I feel his sharp toenails in my hand.

"Another problem for all the species out here is that the nitrogen from the fertilizers the sugar industry uses makes the saw grass grow much denser, and in deeper water, impenetrable stands of cattails. That makes it hard for everything to find food."

I slide the bird out of my pocket and cup a hand over his back. His tiny heart flutters against my palm. I glance at the backs of the other kids' heads. I'm tempted to say "watch this," but decide I don't want to share with them.

Mr. Vickers glances at me. I hesitate, then decide that he won't be mad that I disobeyed the ranger. I un-cup my hands and hold the bird up for him to see. He nods. The bird doesn't move. For a full twenty seconds, he sits there looking at freedom. I wonder if he thinks it's another illusion, like the reflection of a tree in the window. I even touch the top of his head, where the feathers he left on the window came from. He still doesn't move. Maybe something's broken so he can't fly.

"Oh my God!" Courtney cries and grabs the arm of the boy sitting next to her. "There's a snake."

I look where they are pointing and feel the bird leave my hand.

"Is it a cottonmouth?" Adam says.

My warbler lands on the ground a few feet away at the side of the road and just sits there. I look from it to the fat black snake and feel myself shudder. I don't like snakes, and this one is creeping me out by zigzagging right toward us—and my bird.

"Looks like it," Mr. Vickers answers. He's seen where the warbler landed and is watching too.

Adam's hand is waving. Mr. Vickers points to him. "Yes, Philip?"

Philip, not Adam.

"Is its bite always fatal?" he asks.

The snake slows, then stops. Its forked black tongue slides out.

"No," Mr. Vickers says, "but it's a good question."

"Oh," one of the girls says. "There's another one of those little yellow birds."

The snake is maybe two yards away. Its head turns toward the warbler, and its tongue slides in and out twice before it moves again. It's seen the warbler and is headed right for him.

I clap my hands together, and the bird bolts into the air.

"Bummer." One of the boys gives me a dirty look.

Mr. Vickers smiles, then turns and nods for the driver to move on. I like him best of all my teachers. He has red hair, a gazillion freckles, and lots of wrinkles. His smile crinkles his face.

"So?" Philip says. "Is its bite always fatal?"

"It depends on the size of the person bitten, how much venom is injected, and whether there is treatment nearby," Mr. Vickers says. "I don't want you to be freaked out by snakes. Most are not poisonous. I just want to scare you enough to make you think about where you're walking. This field trip is not a stroll through the shops at Dadeland. In the water, there are cottonmouth moccasins and alligators. Coral snakes and scorpions hide under logs, pygmy rattlesnakes enjoy sunning themselves on the levees, and diamondbacks prefer the pinelands. No place is completely safe."

The backs of my knees tingle. What—I wonder yet again—am I doing in this hot, hideous place, and nearly ground-level with things that want to kill and eat you? Why would anyone ever want to come here?

. . .

The observation tower is a concrete spiral that curls up and around a central core. The map the ranger gave us says it's sixty-five feet tall. The boys push and shove as they race each other up the ramp to the top. The four other girls trudge after them, and I bring up the rear.

From the top, the view is 360 degrees and the same scene at every degree: saw grass puncturing the surface of a continuous sheet of water as far as I can see in any direction. The only break in the monotony is an occasional clump of trees. Even in the ninety-eight-degree heat, I feel a sudden chill prickle my skin. The sameness is frightening—a wasteland covered by a shallow layer of scummy water. I wonder how the animals find their way around without anything, anywhere, that looks even a little different from any other thing.

The tower is on an island with a canal nearly all the way around the building. The deep water, edged by cat-tails, is full of fish. A great blue heron stands ankle-deep in the water, staring down as if in a trance. Mr. Vickers points out a green-backed heron, looking hump-shouldered with its head drawn in tightly between its wings, but I can't take my eyes off the alligators. They are enormous things, basking in the sun like lumpy, gray logs. There are five of them, one of which is sleeping with its mouth wide open, exposing a pale pink throat and lots of big, round teeth.

On top of the tower there is a nice breeze. I lean with my elbows spread apart on the railing so my underarms get maximum exposure to the wind. We all smell of sweat and Deep Woods Off, which keeps the mosquitoes from biting but not from whining nearby, searching for an unprotected square inch of skin.

The boys are daring each other to go down and pet a gator. Two of them pretend to drag Courtney, who screams in mock terror, to the edge as a sacrifice. I stand off to one side, watching, kind of smiling. I wouldn't want Mr. Vickers to think I'm as silly as they are, but I don't want the others to think I'm a stick-in-the-mud, either.

The girls take turns taking pictures of themselves with their cell phones held high, so that the alligators are in the picture too. I have a Tracfone for emergencies. It doesn't take pictures, but I can't imagine a phone could take a picture as good as Dad's Leica.

"I have my dad's camera," I say. "Would you like me to take your picture all together?"

Brittany gives me a look like I've just asked them for a blood donation, but the lead Amanda says yes. They line up against the wall, their arms around each other's waists, and flash their brilliant, bleached white teeth at me.

"How old is that thing?" Courtney says.

"It's a *1952* Leica," I say with pride as I turn the focus wheel, bringing the eight of them down to four.

Courtney puts her hand behind Brittany's head to give her horns. "Does it take color pictures?"

"Sure." I take the picture. "I'll have a copy made for each of you."

"Whatever," the other Amanda says.

The boy who wanted to see the moccasin eat the warbler takes a quarter from his pocket and throws it at a gator. It misses. He digs for another. Philip and two of the other boys root in their pockets for coins, wind up, and pitch them in unison so they rain down on one of the gators.

Mr. Vickers sees them and explodes. "If I see one more thing like that, I'll call your parents to come get you, and you *will* receive a failing grade for the semester. Is that clear? If you're going to act like children, you should be home with your mommies and daddies."

Another tram arrives, this one full of tourists. Mr. Vickers, still plenty mad, herds us down the ramp. I lag behind, hoping he'll notice that I'm not part of the group he's mad at.

I take a last look at the scene below in time to see the great blue heron strike and skewer a fish. I raise the camera as the bird turns and takes a step up onto the grass. I turn the focus wheel at the same instant the surface of the water erupts. An alligator, mouth open, launches itself out of the water, catches the heron by a leg, and drags it flapping, but unable to squawk because of the fish impaled on its beak, back into the water. Mud boils as the gator drags it under and spins beneath the surface.

I guess I screamed, because the entire class charges back up the ramp, but by the time they reach the railing, it's over. Muddy water rolls into the cattails, wave after wave, but there's nothing else to see. Nature has taken its course.

"What happened?" Philip asks.

"A gator killed that beautiful heron."

"Cool. Did you get a picture of it?"

"I don't know."

"Well, look."

"This is a film camera. I won't know until I get it developed."

"Boy, that's a bummer."

3

Our destination is the Loop Road Environmental Center. We pull in a little after one. I'm waiting for the others to gather their stuff when through the front windshield I see a guy. He's in a shed beyond the screened-in building marked Dining Hall, working on the engine of a small airboat: one with two seats, not benches like the one at the Miccosukee place. He turns to watch the bus unload, and I guess he's about fifteen. He's tall—taller than the boys on this trip, and a lot cuter. His hair is straight, dark brown with long bangs that fall over one eye. He pushes them aside and shields his eyes against the sun.

I watch him until everyone else gets off, then I step down and look around, smiling as if I'm happy to be here. I wait a moment before I let myself glance in his direction. He's moved into the sunlight and is staring at me. I'm getting used to that, but his is a nice kind of stare, and I feel the blood rush to my face. I turn away, hoist my duffel bag, and walk straight toward our assigned cabin. Just before I start up the steps, I sneak a final peek. He's working on the airboat again, so his back is to me.

The cabin is pitch black compared to outside, which means I have to stand in the doorway and wait for my eyes to adjust. The other girls were shrieking and laughing when I came up the steps, but now they stop and stare.

"What?" I throw my duffel and sleeping bag onto an upper bunk by the door, since they've taken all the bottom bunks.

"Nothing," one of the Amandas says. She's giving Brittany a French braid.

This Amanda is the bell-cow. Mom says in every herd there's a lead cow, and they put a bell on her so when she moves and her bell rings the others follow. Mom says I should try to make friends with the bell-cows at school. I'm not having much luck with that.

They're in their bras and panties, changing into designer swamp-tromping outfits for this afternoon's field trip. I don't feel like getting undressed in front of them, so I go back outside to sit on the top step to wait. They start to whisper as soon as I'm out the door. I can't make out what they're saying except that's it about me.

I'm plucking leaves off the vine that's growing up the banister when they come out in an all-blonde triangle—

the bell-cow in the lead, followed by the other Amanda, Brittany and Courtney. Courtney bumps me as they troop down the stairs but doesn't say sorry, kiss my butt or anything. The idea of an entire weekend trapped here with them makes me want to scream or cry or both. They glance back and giggle. I tell myself I don't care enough about them to get my feelings hurt. I only wish it worked that way.

Mr. Vickers told us to meet in front of the dining hall at two for the field trip to a sanctuary across the road to see the endangered banded tree snail. It makes me feel sorrier for myself to know that even snails have a safe haven.

I come out of the hot cabin in a pair of my mother's shorts, one of my brother's T-shirts, and the long-sleeved denim shirt of my dad's tied around my waist. The AABCs watch me cross the yard with their heads bunched together like they have magnets for brains.

I must be the last one, because Mr. Vickers smiles and starts walking toward the gate. The others form a clump behind him as we cross the Loop Road and enter the sanctuary.

The trail is narrow and mostly crushed shell like the levees are made of. The low spots are muddy from the recent rains but easy to step over or around. We form a single file behind Mr. Vickers, the boys in the front, the AABCs, then me. Mr. Vickers is using binoculars to try to find a snail.

"This is a hardwood hammock," he says. "And these snails are arboreal except when depositing their eggs in leaf mulch. Who can tell me what arboreal means?"

I know the answer is up trees, but my hands are busy trying to wave off our welcoming committee. I didn't soak myself with bug spray again after changing clothes, so the mosquitoes are biting through my T-shirt. I untie Dad's shirt and put it on, which doesn't protect my bare legs. The whining around my face makes me feel panicky. They're even biting my eyelids.

The bell-cow holds a low branch aside for the other Amanda and Brittany. Brittany takes it and holds it for Courtney, who holds it for me. Fool that I am, I move faster to catch up and say thanks at the instant she smiles and lets it go. It hits me in the forehead and across my left eye, which stings and begins to tear.

"Oops. Sorry," Courtney says. The AABs laugh and pat her back when she catches up with them.

I'm not sure which is worse, the mosquitoes or the AABCs. I cover my stinging, watering eye with my hand, turn, and retrace the path until I'm out on the road again but still engulfed in a swirling cloud of insects. I start to run, but the mosquitoes follow me across the yard and up the cabin steps. I'm nearly in tears by the time I burst through the screen door and start to rip through my duffel bag, looking for my can of Deep Woods Off. I spray my face, hair, arms and legs. It's bitter on my lips and stings where the branch hit me across the face—just the excuse I need to sit down heavily on a lower bunk and cry so hard I start to hiccup.

I lie down and try to sleep, but it's too hot inside the cabin and the thought that the AABCs could be back at any minute drives me outside again. There was a red squirrel in the yard when we drove in, much prettier than the scrawny gray ones we have in Miami, so I take the Leica with me.

From the direction of the shed I hear a whirring, then the sputter of the airboat engine. I hang the camera around my neck and drift that direction, looking up into the branches of the oaks for the squirrel. Just past the last cabin, I spot it jamming acorns into its cheeks. I bring the camera to my eye and start to focus the lens.

"They're tame enough to take peanuts from your hand."

I whirl around.

"Sorry. Didn't mean to scare you."

The boy's wiping his hands on a dirty towel.

"You didn't." I'm tempted to say he'd have to get in line if he wants to be one of the things I'm scared of out here, but I don't want him to think I'm a wimp. "You just startled me, that's all."

"Good. You're one in a million then. Most people get real jumpy when they're in the Everglades, thinking there's something deadly behind every blade of grass."

"Isn't there?" I wait a second for his reaction, then smile.

He laughs.

It's a great laugh.

"There's nothing to be afraid of if you just watch where you're walking and don't turn nothing over with your bare hands."

I'm so used to Mom correcting my grammar I almost say, "*anything* over." Instead I look at his filthy feet. "You're not even wearing shoes."

"'Cause I watch where I'm walking." He comes forward and sticks out his hand. "Name's Andy."

In spite of how black with oil his hand is, I take it. "I'm Sarah. Sarah Emerson."

It's silly, but for a moment, I have to fight the urge to say thank you. For the first time since I got on the bus this morning, someone besides Mr. Vickers is being nice to me.

"Pretty name."

"I guess. It was my grandmother's."

"Mine's really Andrew Johnson Malone. Dad's a Civil War nut." He nods toward the Confederate flag hanging on the back wall of the shed.

I'd noticed it earlier from the bus, but I didn't want to assume anything. "That's not a bad name," I say. "Maybe you're lucky he favored the South. You could be named Tecumseh Sherman Malone."

He laughs, and I feel myself blush. I'm not used to having people think I'm funny. "Do you live here?"

"Yeah." He points to the small house in the southeast corner of the property. "My parents kind of manage the place. What happened to your face?"

I touch the welt on my forehead. "I ran into a tree limb."

He looks genuinely concerned. "Want me to get you some Bactine?"

"It's fine." I move my head, and he drops his hand. "What are you doing to that airboat?"

"Trying to fix it before Dad gets back from Miami. I was running it the other day and blew a gasket. He's going to be pissed 'cause the last time I had it out, I did that." He smiles sheepishly and points to the big patch on the bow. "Hit a tree stump."

Since I've never seen an airboat up close, I walk into the shed for a better look. The boat part is aluminum, about fourteen feet long, five feet wide, and flat on the bottom. Mounted on a scaffolding-like framework of metal bars, a few feet in from the stern, is a car engine, which turns a two-blade wooden propeller. A wire cage covers the engine, the propeller, and two vertical rudders. Also mounted on the metal framework is a small square platform with a seat bolted to it, and below it is another seat for a passenger. I know the top one is the driver's since that's where the key is to turn on the engine, but there's nothing that looks like a steering wheel.

"How do you steer it?"

Andy steps up on the trailer tire, then onto the platform and sits in the driver's seat. "These are the controls. This stick..." he touches the right one, "is the throttle, and this one is how you steer." He moves the left stick back and forth, which swings the rudders from side to side.

"I've never been in an airboat, but it looks like fun."

"If I get it running, I'll take you for a ride."

"Where do you take it?"

"I usually put in just west of the Forty-Mile Bend. That's where you turned off the trail to come here."

"How do you get it there?"

"Hook the trailer to that truck." He nods toward the old Dodge parked beside the shed. "And drive it over."

"You drive? How old are you?"

"Fifteen. You?"

"Almost fourteen. So you don't have a driver's license."

"Nobody pays attention to stuff like that out here. Besides, it's only out the Loop and another mile on the highway. I've been driving since I could reach the pedals."

There are a couple small branches caught in the wire cage near his head. Andy pulls them out, then climbs down and starts cleaning out the leaves and twigs that litter the floor of the airboat.

"It sounds like fun, but there are field trips all day tomorrow, then back to Miami on Sunday." I lean in and pick up the floor on my side.

"I could show you more of the Everglades in an hour than you'll see on a dozen field trips, and without getting your feet wet." He glances at my sandals. "Hope you've got something else to wear."

"I do, but why?"

"To slog in."

"What does that mean?" I don't like the sound of the word.

"The first field trip tomorrow is a wet one. They take you for a little walk in water about up to your chest."

"What about alligators and snakes?"

"They post watchers. My parents, when they're home, do that sometimes."

The last thing I want to do is actually get into the water. "Well, I don't know."

"What don't you know?"

"If I should go with you or not."

"I just offered 'cause you said you'd never been. What's the harm? I know my track record don't look too good, but I'm really careful." He glances at the shiny patch on the airboat. "Besides, you may never get another chance, except with a bunch of tourists."

"Well . . ." I think of Amanda bragging about having her mother's Visa card. It would be worth it just to see her face.

"Mom's a midwife, but if she don't run off to deliver a baby, I could get her to make us a picnic, and I'll take you to this really cool camp."

"You may not even get it fixed before we have to go back to Miami."

"If you say yes, I'll have more incentive." He smiles. He has straight teeth and very green eyes.

I pretend to think about it for a minute. I can say no, and spend the whole weekend with the AABCs looking down their pug noses at me, or go and maybe have some fun.

I glance at the moth-eaten Confederate flag. "What would your dad say?"

"I don't really care what he'd say. Are you good with that?" His eyes spark like my asking opens up other stuff with his father.

"I guess I am if you are."

"So is that a yes?"

I nod. "But don't tell anybody. I'm not sure what excuse I'll give my teacher."

"You'll think of something."

"Okay, then." I look around. "I'll need to wait until after they leave on their field trip."

"I'll get it all set up, and we'll roll out of here right behind them."

"Is there anything I can do to help?"

"Nah." He grins. "I about had it done anyway."

I walk back to my cabin, smiling to myself. This weekend may not be a total loss after all.

DAY TWO

4

Early the next morning, the noise of the other girls getting ready for the field trip to the Fakahatchee Strand finally wakes me, but it takes someone poking me before I roll over and rub my eyes.

"You coming?" the bell-cow asks.

The others are waiting for her on the porch. They look like swamp Barbies, all dressed in khakis. I'd love to be a fly on the wall when they find out they're going to get those cute little outfits all wet and muddy.

I shake my head. "I have cramps." I've always liked the sound of that as an excuse for getting out of things you don't want to do, even though I've never had my period. I rub my stomach and squint as if I'm in pain.

"Whatever."

I roll on my back and stare up at the cobwebby ceiling.

"Have fun." I turn my face to the wall so she won't see me grin.

"Is she going?" One of them asks.

"No. She's *sick*." Amanda's voice is sneery.

"Big loss," Brittany says.

"What about our stuff?" Courtney says.

"She wouldn't dare," the bell-cow says.

I close my eyes. Maybe—with some luck—they'll get eaten by alligators.

I make myself breathe deeply and think about the day ahead instead of those twits. I listen to the shouts and racket of the kids boarding the bus and try to imagine the fun I'm going to have with the added bonus of not having them treat me like a leper.

"Sarah?"

Mr. Vickers is at the screen door.

I try to look sick as I turn to face him. "Yes sir?"

"Amanda says you're not feeling well."

"No sir."

"Shall I call someone to come get you?"

"No," I say, maybe a little too quickly. "I'll be fine by this afternoon."

"We'll be back for lunch."

"Okay."

He stands for a moment, looking at me through the screen. "You're a smart girl, Sarah. In the long run, that's all that will matter. Do you understand?"

"Yes sir."

"I hope you feel better."

A tear forms in my right eye, then rolls out and down my cheek into my ear. I wish what he said was true, but either way, he's too nice to lie to. "Thank you," I say, but am just ready to say that I probably feel okay enough to go when he turns and goes down the steps.

The air is already beginning to warm in the cabin, but the slick surface of the sleeping bag feels cool against my legs. After I hear the last bus leave, I get up, stand on the ladder, and rifle through my duffel bag, trying to decide what to wear. I wonder if an airboat ride counts as a date?

Andy told me to wear long pants and a long-sleeved shirt to protect against cuts from the sharp-edged saw grass, so I lay out a pair of jeans and Dad's shirt, but by the time I wash my face and brush my teeth, it's too hot to stay covered up. I put on Mom's shorts with an assortment of zippered pockets, but they are too baggy and make my legs look like sticks. I take those off and put on a pair of blue shorts. I choose a yellow T-shirt and tie my Dad's old shirt around my waist by the sleeves.

Andy also told me to bring a cap, but the only one I have is a sweat-stained, high-profile, half mesh, Alabama Jack's fishing cap of Dad's. I dig deep into my duffel bag and find a bandana. Last night, at the after-dinner lecture and slide presentation, Courtney wore a bandana with the ends pulled through a soda-can ring. I hate to admit it, but she looked kind of cool. I rummage in the cabin trash for an empty can, find one, and break off the ring.

Yesterday, at the Miccosukee Indian restaurant, the tourists on the airboat ride were weighted down with multiple cameras and bulky binoculars hanging like so many anchors around their necks. I don't want to look like them, but I don't want to miss anything either. I seal Dad's camera into a large Ziploc bag to insure it doesn't even get splashed, then put it and my binoculars in the bottom zippered compartment of my backpack, add my hairbrush, a tube of lip gloss, a mirror, a single can of mosquito repellent (though I have two with me), and my brother's treasured Swiss Army knife, which he had trouble letting go of after he offered to loan it to me. I add a tube of sunscreen and put the potato chips and apples that I picked up last night at dinner into the top half of the pack.

There's a foggy mirror on the wall between two of the bunks. It has a full-length crack in it that makes my right half look slightly shorter than my left half. I've got long legs, the too-wide shoulders of a swimmer, and no breasts to speak of. Mom says that's a good thing. She says young girls with breasts have them from eating fast-food hamburgers all the time, which come from cattle pumped full of hormones. "When you get your period, breasts will follow," she says.

"Looking good," I say to the two halves of my image in the mirror, then turn sideways to admire my outfit. Real outdoorsy, I decide before pulling the string to the light bulb.

Andy is finished washing the airboat and has backed the old Dodge up to the trailer. He smiles as I come across the yard. "Sleep well?"

"Not really," I say. "Too hot. What can I do to help?"

"Not a thing. We're ready to rock and roll." He looks at my feet. "What are those for?"

I'm wearing bright yellow rubber boots, which look kind of hot with my shorts and match my T-shirt. "Making doubly sure my feet stay dry."

"Uh huh," he says.

My stomach growls.

"Hungry, huh?"

"Starved. I didn't eat breakfast."

"We can stop at the Miccosukee Restaurant for pumpkin bread. Will that hold you 'til lunch?"

"I can't stay out for lunch. They're all coming back here to eat, so I have to be back by noon, okay?"

"That's a bummer. If we stop for breakfast, it won't give us much time."

"We don't have to stop. I've got some chips and two apples."

"Well, I've got cheese and Gatorade. Will that be enough?"

"Plenty."

Andy goes around and opens the truck door for me, then holds his hand out to help me into the cab.

I've seen Dad do this for Mom. "Thanks," I say.

. . .

When I was younger, Dad used to take me fishing in the Keys. Our boat was only fourteen feet, too small for him to take both me and my brother at the same time, so I only got to go every other weekend. When Andy asks me to hold the bowline and walk down the ramp while he backs the trailer toward the water, I think about those trips with Dad. I do like I used to do for him, and when the airboat begins to float, I guide it off the trailer. Andy drives the truck back up the ramp and parks it on the grassy strip between the road and the canal.

I hold the boat tight to the shoreline. Cars whiz by on the highway, and I imagine they envy me. I think about the Barbies on the hot bus ride to the Fakahatchee. I really wouldn't have minded seeing it if it didn't include riding the bus with them, and getting in the water.

Andy asks what I'm smiling about. He's carrying a ratty-looking blue bag with a Pan Am logo on it and a small cooler.

"I guess I'm glad to be here and not on the bus with the others."

"I forgot to ask. How'd you get out of going?"

I put the back of my hand to my forehead and scrunch up my eyes. "Don't I look sick to you?"

"Very. I'm not sure we should even go."

I pretend to kick him, then start to hand off the rope. "Wait. I want to take your picture."

"Only if I can take yours."

"Okay, though I'm not sure I'll show either of them to my parents. I'm not too keen on them ever finding out about this."

I hold the airboat in place with my foot on the rope and take Andy's picture sitting in the driver's seat. We switch places after I show him how to focus.

"Cool camera," he says and snaps my picture with my hand on the throttle.

"My mother wanted to kill Dad for buying it, but he never spends money on himself, so she finally forgave him. I still can't believe he loaned it to me." I put it back in the Ziploc and seal the bag.

Andy puts one leg in and pushes us off with the other foot. He takes a long-sleeved shirt from the Pan Am bag and puts it on over his T-shirt, then climbs past me to his seat. He puts a key in the ignition, pumps the rubber-buttoned choke three times, and starts to turn the key. "Oops," he says.

"What?"

"Nothing. We need ear protection. Hand me the flight bag will you?" He'd left it on the deck beneath my seat. When we get going, if I tilt my head back at all, it will rest against his knees. I like the thought of that.

I get down, hand the bag up to him, and climb back into my seat.

"Here," Andy says. "You wear these ear guards, and I'll wear the plugs."

"Do we need these?" I turn them over in my hand. They're the same as people working around airplanes wear, bulbous and ugly, with a wide, tight band that will mash my hair. I hand them back. "I'll take the plugs," I say. "You're closer to the engine."

We swap, and Andy waits for me to get the plugs into my ears before he turns the key. The engine starts with an explosion of smoke, and I grab the sides of my seat. There's nothing else to hold on to, except maybe his feet. I turn to watch the propeller in the cage behind him spin first one way, then the other, until its two blades blur. I face forward and push the plugs deeper into my ears.

The noise increases as Andy gives the engine more gas, and we begin to skim across the surface of the canal like sliding on ice. Birds lift into the air; turtles, sunning on logs, drop into the water. Basking alligators in assorted sizes launch themselves into the canal.

We're going fast when Andy makes a skidding left turn off the canal through a break in a stand of cattails.

I scream when we turn, though I wouldn't have if I could have helped myself. It doesn't matter. I can't hear my own voice over the roar of the engine, so I'm pretty sure Andy didn't hear me. I tilt my head back and grin up at him.

I thought it would feel like riding in a convertible, but it doesn't. Not anything like that at all. The sensation is of moving through the landscape at a high speed while perched on top of a pole. We are on a trail of open water and going so fast it feels like we're skimming above the surface on a pocket of air, until he turns us into the saw grass and I feel the tug of it beneath the boat. My arms and legs sting, which makes me think I'm getting pelted with insects, but when I look there are tiny cuts and flecks of blood. That's why Andy told me to wear long sleeves. The airboat is like a lawn mower, and the bits of saw grass fly up and cut my arms and legs. We're going so fast I'm only able to undo the sleeves of Dad's shirt and slip my arms inside. It makes me feels hog-tied, but warmer and more protected.

The floor of the airboat is accumulating critters. Little green tree frogs—a half dozen at least—hop about. They must be confused and scared; one minute they're clinging to a cattail blade, and the next they're whizzing along as if captured by aliens. Every tall stand we plowed through adds to the collection: a few more frogs and a dozen more spiders. The tiny spiders are everywhere, but unlike the disoriented frogs, they immediately set about building new webs. I want to brush away the ones that have landed on me, but it would mean letting go of the sides of my seat. Instead I try not to think about them and soon begin to admire their focus. The Pan Am bag, a long pole, the gas can, and the cooler are all being webbed to the deck with hopeful little strands of silk.

Off to our left is a strip of dry land with a few low shrubs and a tree or two. It's on the way to becoming a tree island—a hammock—according to the lecture we had last night. Andy veers toward it. "Hang on," he shouts, his mouth warm next to my ear.

My heart races as he takes direct aim at the patch of dry land. When we hit, the airboat slows and looks as if it's going to stop, but Andy gives it more gas and uses the stick to flap the rudders from side to side. The rear of the airboat fishtails. We are nearly to the far edge when it stops completely.

"Go stand in the bow," Andy yells in my ear.

I climb down and step cautiously through the frogs to the front of the boat. Andy opens the throttle full blast and uses the stick to flap the rudders again. The boat moves sluggishly until it lurches off the edge and back into the shallow water and thick, short saw grass. After I climb back into my seat, Andy runs the airboat in a tight circle, over and over, until he's flattened the saw grass into what looks like a crop circle. He moves the throttle to neutral.

"Why'd you do that?" I ask.

"I thought maybe you'd like to run her, and this gives us a launch pad. Thick grass, water hyacinths and mud can stop an airboat, not to mention dry land." He grins.

"Can I really drive?"

"Sure. Nothing to it, just don't try to show off." His eyes sparkle.

He steps down to help me climb into his seat. "The most important thing is how you steer. Push the stick right, you go left, left for right. You'll get the hang of it."

Right away, I give it too much gas, pull back, and end up in neutral again. I test the rudders, which sways the back end like a duck walking. As I get a feel for the boat, I ease the throttle forward, adding gas slowly until we're going pretty fast, but not fast enough to be scary.

A couple of times, Andy had raced at a solid-looking wall of cattails, or a dense stand of saw grass, and hadn't even slowed down. Just when it looked like we'd fly up the side and flip over, the boat flattened a path through the center. It was exciting, so I search the horizon for a stand of cattails to hit. When I see one, I slow to make the turn toward it.

"Where you going?" Andy shouts.

I point. "Those cattails."

He laughs and gives me a thumbs-up.

As we barrel toward the stand, I'm suddenly afraid but fight the urge to veer off. Instead, I stare at the cattails until it feels like we're standing still and the bank of green is in a headlong rush to consume us. In a second or two we will be swallowed up by a sea of green stalks. I see a duck lift off the water in front of us just before I squeeze my eyes shut and hit the wall of cattails. I feel the tug of the thick stalks beneath us, then the surge as the airboat comes out into water on the other side. I open my eyes, pull back on the throttle, and laugh.

Andy's looking at something; then, without a word, he hops over the side. The water's only knee-deep as he wades to the edge of the cattails. He leans over with his hands on his hips. He reaches for something, and when he turns, in each hand is a dead baby duck.

5

"It's my fault." Andy reaches up and turns off the ignition. "All sorts of animals live and hide in the cattails and saw grass. I should have told you. You didn't know." He lifts an arm to pitch the first one overboard.

"Don't," I cry.

"Why?"

"We need to bury them."

"Bury them? Look where we are."

"We'll take them to wherever we're going and bury them there."

"Why?"

"I don't know. So nothing eats them."

"What have you got against letting the dead feed the living? Something should eat them," he says. "Otherwise their death is wasted."

"It's just not right to throw them away."

"So you want to have a little funeral?" He smiles.

I feel my cheeks burn. He's laughing at me. "I just want to bury them."

"Cover them with dirt and let the worms eat 'em, huh? How dumb is that? It goes against nature's plan . . ."

This reminds me of what the ranger said about the warbler. I raise my hands to shut Andy up. "Stop with that let-nature-take-its-course thing."

"You're in the wrong place to feel that way."

"I don't care. I killed them, and we're going to bury them."

Andy looks at the duckling in his left hand. I thought I saw something, too. "Did it just move?"

"I think it did." He hands it up to me, and puts his ear to the breast of the other one. Its little head slides off the side of his hand and dangles limply. "This one's neck is broken."

The one cupped in my hands opens its eyes. "I think this one is okay. Just stunned." I smile. "Maybe we can find its mother."

Andy snorts. "That duck's a zillion miles from here." He puts his hand out to help me down. "What are you going to do with it?"

I'm surprised he asks. "Take it back with us."

"You gonna raise it in your bathtub?"

"Can't you keep it? You live out here."

"It will be imprinted."

"What does that mean?"

"It will be tame, not afraid of people. That's not good for a wild thing."

"Well, what would you do with it?"

He rolls his eyes like he knows he's wasting his breath. "Put it overboard for something to catch and eat."

"That's sick. There's no way I'm leaving it here." I look at the dead one, lying on the cooler lid. "You can put that one over the side if you want to."

"Naw. There are gators where we're going. I'll feed it to one of them."

"You will not. Give it to me."

I pick it up. Its eyes are dull, black slits. I feel awful about killing it and stroke its downy yellow belly and touch its rubbery little bill. "I'm sorry," I say, then lob it into the cattails. "I don't want to see anything else eaten by a gator."

"What'd you see eaten?"

"A heron."

"What kind of heron?"

"A great blue."

"Where'd you see that?"

"From the observation tower in Shark Valley."

"Cool."

Boys.

The duckling in my hand tries to leap down, but I catch it midair, then carefully let it go on the floor of the boat. It pads around, peeping like a baby chick, calling for its mother, I guess. It steps on one of the last remaining frogs, most of which have escaped over the side while we've been sitting here. When the frog wriggles out from beneath its webbed foot, the duckling falls on its butt, then can't get its feet under itself. Andy and I laugh, but I can't help feeling sad, like this is another reason I shouldn't be here. If we weren't out here messing around where we don't belong, the little thing would still be with its mother.

Andy climbs back up to his seat, and I catch the baby duck before he starts the engine. It squirms, trying to find solid ground with its flapping feet. I hand it to Andy while I put on Dad's shirt, button it up, and tuck the tail into my shorts. When he hands the duckling back, I put it down the front of my shirt. Its toenails scratch my stomach as it tries to climb back out, but when I cup my hands over it, it calms down and lies quietly.

Andy points to a tree island in the distance. "That's where we're headed."

Good. I'm starving.

. . .

The entrance to the camp is invisible. I hold my breath when Andy turns us and, without even slowing down, takes aim at a narrow channel through a stand of cattails. Only when we see the trail is blocked by tree limbs does he cut the motor.

"Are you sure there's a cabin in there?" I already don't like this place.

"Last time I looked." He's busy breaking away the branches that snag the propeller cage. When we're through the densest part, he pulls the airboat, hand over hand, along the channel until we clear the tree limbs and glide into a man-made pond that is right out of the movie *The Creature from the Black Lagoon* that I saw on the Turner Classic Movie channel.

Oh my God, I'm thinking when Andy says, "Kind of pretty, ain't it?"

It's the ugliest place I've ever seen. The cabin is nothing but plywood covered with black tar paper, the pond water is black, and the mud at the edge is black. The cypress trees are so dense no light gets through. I'm totally creeped out even before I see the alligator. It had been asleep on the muddy bank, but now its eyes are open and staring at us. The hair on my arms stands up as I watch about fourteen feet of lumpy gray reptile slide lazily into the water and disappear. The tower at Shark Valley was over twice as tall as the high-dive platform at school. Looking at huge gators from there was one thing, but being this close to one that is now somewhere beneath us is freaking me out. I know it can still see us, and all I can think about is seeing that gator at Shark Valley explode out of the water, launch itself at the heron, and drag the poor thing under. I start to shiver.

I'm so focused on trying to see where the gator is that I nearly jump out of my skin when Andy swings down from his perch. He grabs the pole and pushes us toward the rotting dock.

"So what d'ya think?"

"Can we go now?"

"What d'ya mean go? We just got here."

"Didn't you see that gator?"

"Sure, but he's not going to bother us. Come on." Andy hops across to what's left of an old dock and holds out his hand.

About every other plank is missing, and where the dock ends there is a double row of equally rotten boards set side-by-side on top of what looks like ankle-deep mud. Where the mud ends, the boards zigzag through knee-deep weeds. *One in a million, ha!* I'm with the other 999,999 who are afraid of everything out here. I can already imagine feeling the first of the bloodthirsty ticks waiting to crawl up my bare, saw-grass–cut, chill-bump–covered legs.

I fight down the urge to beg him to leave right this second, hold the duckling steady against my stomach, and take his hand. His palm is warm and calloused like my dad's, and I'm suddenly and oddly homesick.

I step across to the dock and follow Andy along the plank walkway, holding onto a belt-loop of his jeans. I will myself not to think about what is living beneath each termite-eaten plank. One thing Floridians know practically from birth, even city kids like me, is to never turn over a log or board—the dark, damp places where coral snakes and scorpions like to hide.

The walkway parallels the side of the shack, makes a right turn, and ends at the remnants of steps. The shack, like the dining hall and the cabins at the Loop Road Environmental Center, is perched on concrete blocks, which makes me think the water must get a lot higher than it is right now.

"Does someone live here?" I can't imagine.

"This is a hunting camp. It belongs to someone, but all the camps out here are left open for anyone to use."

That's big of them, I think to myself. What's to lock? What's to steal?

From the front of the cabin, an overgrown trail meanders a short distance to the edge of the woods and ends at a plywood outhouse that someone has decorated by painting a quarter-moon on the door. It's a facility I'm in desperate need of. I get as far as the door, but I'm afraid to open it.

"Go in the woods," Andy suggests, putting the cooler on a makeshift picnic table: two sawhorses and a sheet of plywood set between two decaying tree-stump stools.

I glance at the dark tangle of trunks and vines behind the outhouse. "No way, and I can't go in there either unless you'll check it for things first."

He comes, opens the door, steps inside, and lets the door smack shut behind him.

I wait.

"What are you doing?" I say.

"Peeing," he answers.

"I was first."

"Not through the door, you weren't." The door swings open, and Andy comes out carrying a very large, colorful snake.

I scream and run from him down the trail, holding the duckling against my stomach.

"It's only a corn snake," Andy says, as if that will make a difference.

"Don't come near me with that thing," I plead. "I hate snakes."

Andy stands stock-still. "I hadn't planned to," he says. "I don't want to scare the snake."

"Very funny."

"Why do you hate snakes?"

"They're slimy." I shudder. I have no intention of telling him how my brother stood on a ladder in our laundry room, which shares a drop-ceiling with the bathroom, and pitched a snake into the shower with me. He still loves to tell his friends how I took the shower curtain and rod down with me and looked like a cat in a sack trying to get out the door.

"No, they aren't." He drapes it around his neck but keeps a good grip on it right behind its head. "I'll hold her head. Come touch her." He holds its tail out to me.

"No way."

"She's not slimy. She's dry as a bone and cool to the touch."

"I don't care. I don't want to touch her. And how do you know she's a she?"

"I don't think I know you well enough to go into that."

"Whatever." I shrug. "I still don't want to touch her."

"Suit yourself."

"What was she doing in there, anyway?"

"People bring these snakes out and leave them to keep the rats under control. So use the head, then let me put her back."

Gators. Rats. Snakes. What was I thinking, coming out here with him?

If he'd been my brother, he would jump at me with the snake, so I just stand there until he steps off into the weeds and gives me a clear path to the outhouse. He speaks softly to the snake and rubs it under its chin. The snake's forked tongue flicks in and out, which makes my skin tingle with disgust.

Still, I don't trust him, and I scoot by, jerk the outhouse door open, and back in. I close the door, then shoot right back out again. "There's a huge spider-web in there."

"It's way up in the corner."

"But the spider?"

"She won't bother you."

"I can't sit there with a giant spider above my head."

A clear expression of boredom crosses his face. "Pee in the woods then." He strokes the snake and lets its tongue touch his cheek.

I shiver at the thought of a snake's tongue against my cheek, and I know Andy thinks I'm acting like a sissy, but I can't help how sickening this place is. I'm from the city, for God's sake. Why would he think this world of snakes, rats, outhouses, and alligators is an easy adjustment? Tears threaten, so I whirl, snatch the door open, and duck, even though the web is in a corner high above my head. I let the door slam, then look for a lock just in case he decides it would be fun to pitch the snake in here with me. There isn't one. Just a knothole that I can put my finger through to hold the door closed.

The spider, which is about the size of my hand, moves up the web on its long, hairy red legs. I sit kind of sideways over the smelly hole so I can watch it. The duckling waits on the dirt floor, preening its matted belly, wet from my sweat.

"Do you want to see inside the cabin?" Andy asks after he put the snake back in the outhouse.

"Sure." I'm trying to sound brave. The airboat ride was fun—until I killed the duckling—but enough is enough. I just want to go back right now to the Loop Road camp, which is luxury compared to this place. Maybe I could continue to pretend I'm sick for the rest of the day, and tomorrow leave for home without ever seeing another inch of the Everglades.

The cabin has a screened-in porch with most of the screens punched out and a door that sags on its last rusty hinge. When Andy tries to straighten it so it will swing open, the door comes off in his hands. He shrugs, carries it across the porch, and neatly leans it against the wall. The hollow-core wood door to the cabin is warped and rotting from the bottom up. Andy has to shoulder it open like a cop breaking into a suspect's house.

It's pitch black inside. I'm pressed so tight on Andy's heels that my nose brushes his shoulder.

"What's that awful smell?"

"Just a little mold and mouse piss."

A claustrophobic chill sweeps over me. I draw my head in like a turtle, ducking at the sound of feet scurrying across the plywood ceiling.

Andy, with me in lockstep, crosses to the sink, smacks the swollen wooden window with the heel of his hand to break the seal, then props it open with a broom handle. A roach, startled by the sudden flood of light, lifts off the floor and flies toward us. I plaster myself against Andy's back, squeezing a peep out of the duckling in my shirt. The roach hits Andy in the chest. He brushes it off and stomps it.

"I hate roaches." I turn and start for the door, but Andy catches my hand.

"It was a palmetto bug. Come on, don't be such a chicken."

"Roach, palmetto bug, whatever. I hate them both," I snap. "And I'm not a chicken. This place is disgusting."

A cracked porcelain sink is set in an unfinished wooden counter. Above it is the open window, and on either side of the window are bare plank shelves lined with mismatched plastic plates and a couple of bloated, deadly looking cans of pork and beans.

In the center of the room, another table has been created out of two more sawhorses and a split and peeling sheet of plywood. Four rusty metal folding chairs sit at different angles, as if the occupants had left suddenly.

I imagine a fight over cheating at cards and the players leaving to shoot each other in the yard.

In the far corner are two pairs of bunk beds, head to head. Each has a mattress that looks as if it'd been dragged here from the Dade County dump. A filthy pillow lies at the head of each bunk. Towels and army blankets are stacked along a wooden bench attached to the fourth wall of the cabin.

"It's nothing fancy," Andy says. "But . . ."

I burst out laughing.

For a second he looks hurt, then he starts laughing too. "It is only a hunting cabin," he says, lamely, as I wipe tears from my cheeks.

In contrast to the rest of the camp, there's a relatively new wooden swing hanging from a limb of a huge old cypress tree by chains that are beginning to rust. After Andy kicks a picnic-table stump and it crumbles, releasing a swarm of red ants, he takes the cooler to the swing. I pull my shirttail out, catch the duckling, and put it on the ground.

We sit side by side, each eating from our own small bag of potato chips. Half a bar of cheddar cheese waits on Andy's knee to be divided, and an open bottle of Gatorade is jammed in the space between our thighs. I loan Andy my Swiss Army knife to cut the apple into quarters.

"This is a nice knife." He turns it in his hand. His fingernails are dirty, and the cuticles chewed and ragged. "I forgot, there's Spam, too."

"Yuck," I say. "What is Spam, anyway?"

"Ham and something. Salami, I think. Read the can."

"I don't want to even get that close to it." I make a face.

"You'd feel different if you were hungry." Andy hands me a chunk of apple and one of cheese.

"Well, I hope I'm never *that* hungry." I crumble a chip and scatter it at my feet for the duckling.

"It's good fried."

"I doubt it." I take a bite of cheese, then one of apple. They taste good together. "Got any cups?"

"For what?"

I tap the lid of the Gatorade.

"We either have to drink after each other, or . . ." He grins. "I bet there are glasses in the cabin."

"Tough choice." I take a sip from the bottle, wipe the lip, and hand it to him.

He takes it, but just keeps looking at me.

"What?"

"Let's end the germ problem right now." He takes my chin, turns my face, and tries to kiss me.

My stomach does a flip-flop, but I turn my head sharply. "Who said you could do that?"

"I like you," Andy says.

"Well, I might not like you."

"Don't you?"

"I haven't decided yet." I smile.

"Well, decide. I only give airboat rides home to people who like me." He takes a long drink.

"Just turn the bottle," I say.

He wipes the rim and hands it back to me. "So, Emerson, what do you do all day in Miami?"

I take another sip and shrug. "Nothing much. School. Swimming practice. Homework. Play on the computer. You know."

"Sounds like a full and rewarding life."

"What do you do? Gig frogs?"

It came out as a put-down, but before I can apologize, Andy smiles. "School. Gig frogs. You know."

"What is a gig, anyway?"

"A long pole with a miniature pitchfork at the end."

I nod and think of all those cute little green frogs. "Doesn't seem like much of a meal. Their legs are so little."

He looks at me blankly; then it dawns on him. "Not the little green ones. They gig the big bull-frogs and pig frogs."

A picture of a frog run through with tiny, sharp tines, its legs kicking, comes to mind, and I change the subject. "Where *do* you go to school?"

"Naples. Maybe you could come back over someday. Go to a game or a dance with me." He smiles, then adds, "I don't really gig frogs, you know."

When I was little, Mom signed me up for ballet, tap and piano lessons, but I don't know anything about dancing *with* someone. "A game would be fun, but I don't really know how to dance."

"I'm not a very good dancer anyway. Maybe a game, or a movie."

"Sure. I guess." I have a big picture of my parents driving me all the way to Naples and back for a date with Andy, but it's nice to think about anyway. As good-looking and nice as he is, I bet he has lots of friends—especially girlfriends. I take another sip of Gatorade and wipe the rim. I'm just passing it to him when I see the duckling round the side of the cabin.

"Come here little duck, duck." I get up, patting my thigh.

I've only gone a few feet when Andy says, "Oh my God." I freeze, afraid he's seen a rattlesnake or something.

"What?" I cry when he runs past me. "What?" I run after him.

When I catch up, he's standing on the dock, hitting himself in the forehead over and over with the heel of his hand.

My heart is thundering. "What's the matter?"

He drops to his knees on the dock, folds himself in half, locks his hands behind his neck, and starts to rock. "Oh my God. Oh my God."

I can see past him now and bite my fist to keep from screaming. The airboat is gone.

6

My first thought is that it had been stolen, but when Andy sank to his knees on the dock, I see the curved top of the propeller cage arching over the water. One blade sticks up like the arm of a drowning victim, and a few final air bubbles rise to the surface and pop in the rainbow of gas that encircles the cage.

I don't realize I'm crying until he glances at me. For a moment I see the look of anguish in his eyes, then he blinks it away and slips off into the water. I immediately think of the gator. It's still down there somewhere, but Andy wades around, collecting the things that were floating: the pole, the gas can, the Pan Am flight bag, and a single flip-flop. He dumps them at my feet and looks up. "I'm sorry."

Tears stream down my face. "What are we going to do?"

"I'm not sure," he says.

"Can't we tip it over like a canoe and empty the water out?"

I knew that was a stupid question almost the minute I said it, but when Andy snorts "no," it makes me mad. "How did this happen?" I cry.

"I washed it this morning and took the stern plug out so the water would drain. I put the plug on one of the trailer's tires."

"And you forgot it was there?"

"Yeah, I guess."

"Why didn't it sink when we put it in the canal?"

"It takes a while to fill through that little hole." He's standing chest-deep with both hands on the dock, his head down. "And as long as we were moving, water couldn't get in."

I glance at the cabin. There are no power or phone lines. My parents gave me the Tracfone for my birthday, but I didn't bother to bring it. In fact, I've never used it. There's no one to call. "Did you bring your cell?"

He snorts again. "I don't have a cell phone. Even if I did, there are no cell towers out here." He takes a deep breath and looks up at me. "I'm gonna have to walk out."

My turn to snort. "You've got to be kidding? How far is it?"

He shrugs. "'Bout ten miles, I guess."

"Oh." I'm suddenly hopeful. "That's not far." He could go get help and be back in a couple of hours.

Andy gives a short, bitter laugh. "Not on a city side-walk, it ain't."

"How long will it take?"

"Two days, maybe."

"Two days!" My throat closes.

"Maybe three. The water's still pretty high."

"No."

"What do you mean, no?"

"You can't."

"I'll be fine. It's not as bad as it looks." He dips his hand in the water and lets it pour through his fingers.

"Andy, I can't stay here by myself. What happens when it gets dark?"

"You can sleep in the cabin."

A shudder runs through me. "There are rats and *roaches* in there."

"There's nothing out here to hurt you if you stay in the cabin after dark. You may see or hear raccoons, a skunk, or a possum, but nothing dangerous. Plus, you got your buddy there." He nods toward the duckling, which is snuggled against my foot, its head tucked between its shoulder blades. Every few seconds it makes a little peeping sound, as evenly spaced as hiccups.

"Why can't we wait for them to find us?"

"Who's them?"

"Your parents."

"This is Saturday. Dad won't be back until Monday afternoon. Mom left early this morning to help with a baby that's due this weekend. Who knows when she'll be back? There's no one to miss me."

"Well, I'll be missed. They'll be getting back pretty soon, and Mr. Vickers will come to check on me. He'll call my parents as soon as he finds me missing."

"Even so, Sarah, how long will it take anyone to guess where you went? Did you tell any of the other girls you were going out on the airboat with me?"

Tell the AABCs? After they make sure I didn't steal any of their junk, they'll be happy I'm gone. I bite my lip, then shake my head. "Didn't you tell someone?"

"No. Remember? It was our little secret. And what makes you think it will occur to anyone that you might be in the missing airboat, if they even notice it's gone?" Andy hitches himself up on the dock and sits with his legs dangling in the water. He seems unconcerned that the gator has resurfaced and is watching us—just his eyes and two nose-holes above the surface.

"The way I figure it," he says finally, "they may miss you pretty soon, unless they think you've gone for a walk. When they do realize you're gone, they won't know where to start looking. They might think you've been kidnapped or something. It won't occur to anyone that we might be together until one of my parents gets home. In all likelihood, that will be my father late Monday. Best guess is they'll find the boat trailer Monday evening, but too late to start searching. And even then, they won't have a clue which direction I went, or that you're with me. Once they start searching, it could take a week to finally locate us if we stay here. You saw how overgrown this place is. You can't even see it from the air. There's a north-south levee. If I start walking now, I can be on it by Monday, and out by Tuesday morning."

I begin to tremble. Everything he says makes perfect sense. "Maybe the owners will come out to hunt."

"It ain't hunting season, and they haven't been here in months, maybe even years."

"That swing looks pretty new."

"So you think they'll come out to visit it?"

"Don't be mean. I can't stay here alone for a minute, much less for a couple of nights. No way."

He sighs and shrugs. "There's only one other choice then. You have to come with me."

"Are you crazy? I can't swim through that." I point to the pond scum that has drifted in to encircle his legs. "And there are alligators everywhere."

"The gators ain't gonna bother us, and there's no swimming involved. This is the deepest water we'll see. Except for a gator hole once in a while, the water's only a few inches to a foot deep."

"What about water moccasins? Mr. Vickers told us they're aggressive. One swam right at us when we were at Shark Valley."

"We just have to keep our eyes open."

I feel totally exhausted and out of arguments. I put my face in my hands. "I can't stay here alone," I say. "Please, Andy, I can't."

He stands and puts his arms around me. His wet shirt feels cold against the sun-heated skin of my arms. "Then you have to come with me. Those are our only choices. There's no food. We can't last a week or more on swamp water and a can of Spam."

"We can build a fire," I say suddenly. "They'll see the smoke."

"Well, that's a good idea," he says, and strokes my hair. "Of course, we'd need dry wood and dry matches."

"In the cabin?"

"It's been raining almost every day since June. Nothing's dry in that cabin, and there's nobody to see a fire, and if there was, they'd think it was some fisherman cooking dinner. Nobody knows we're missing. You have to remember that. Do you really want to sit here 'til we hear the first airboat or see the first search plane—days, even a week from now?"

"Maybe it won't take that long. We could wait until we hear a plane, rub sticks together like they do on *Survivor* and burn the whole cabin down. They'd see that, wouldn't they?"

"What's *Survivor*?"

"A reality show."

"Is that something on TV?" His tone is curious.

"Don't tell me you've never seen it."

"We don't have a TV."

"If you've never seen it, how do you know that we can't stay right here and survive on berries and stuff until we're found?"

He rolls his eyes.

"I don't think you should make fun of my idea if you've never seen the show. About twenty people get left on an island where they have to fend for themselves for thirty-nine days. They get fires started by rubbing sticks together . . ." *I think. Or do they? I can't remember. Weren't the first competitions always for flints and a machete?*

"Sarah, even if you could start a fire by rubbing wet, green sticks together, which you can't, this place actually belongs to someone—remember? As bad as it is, they might not like us burning it down."

The duckling stands and stretches on one leg, then steps up on my foot and nestles down again. I pick it up and bring it close to my face so the tears I can't control fall and bead on its back.

. . .

Andy goes back to the cabin for the cooler, my backpack, and my shirt, which I left hanging over the back of the swing. I can hear him opening and closing cupboards, but when he comes down the path, all he has is the can of Spam and a butcher knife.

"There's nothing of any use to us in there except this." He holds up the knife.

"What are you doing with that?"

"Just in case." He looks toward the gator at the far end of the pond, then at me. "But if you're staying, I'll leave it, and the Spam, with you." He holds the knife out to me—handle first.

"Andy, please, let's wait until tomorrow. Maybe someone will come by—a fisherman or a frog-gigger."

"No way that's going to happen, Sarah. Have you seen or heard a single airboat all day? We're miles from where the Indians take the tourists." He hands me the Spam, sits on the dock and slips into the water. "I want to get a few hours in before dark."

Dark! The backs of my knees tingle like they do whenever I see someone else's blood. I stare hard at the Spam for a moment, then glance at the gator.

"He's just waiting for us to leave so he can haul back out," Andy says.

"If something got you, no one would ever know what happened to me."

"You should come with me. I'll get us out. I promise."

I think about the few times my family has gone to the beach. Even there, with them on colorful towels nearby, I never went in the water past my knees because it was too silty to see the bottom. I couldn't stand the thought of what I might step on, or what was just beneath the surface looking up. The difference is that at the ocean, I'm pretty sure it was only my imagination; here the danger is real. The gator floats ten yards away, watching.

"I can't," I say. My whole body trembles.

"You have to, Sarah."

I shake my head.

He takes the duckling off the top of my foot and puts it in the water, then takes the backpack out of my hand, unzips it, and drops the Spam inside. He swings the pack around and sticks his arms through the straps.

"It's best this way," he says and holds a hand out to help me off the dock. "You'd never make it here alone."

I know he's right and hate him for it. Hate him so thoroughly I can't speak. I kick my foot like a child, sending the flip-flop spinning.

He looks at me, but says nothing.

"Hand me the flight bag, will you?"

I kick it off the dock, too.

He catches it before it hits the water.

"Are you going to carry that, too?" I ask, wiping tears away with the heels of my hands.

"No. I'm gonna hang it in a tree near the entrance to the channel. If anybody finds it, they'll know this is where we started from, and they'll know we went east."

"How would they know that?" I sniffle.

Andy shakes the bag. Something shifts inside. He unzips it and dumps out the flip-flop that matches the one that has floated across the pond and is bumping against the trunk of a pond-apple tree. "'Cause that's the closest dry land. The levee is due east and much closer than the trail." He holds his hand out again.

I sit down on the edge of the dock, hesitate, then put my feet into the black water. Chill bumps spread up my arms.

The water is to his waist and is covered with a sheet of pale brown scum, which has floated back and encircles his chest.

"I'll throw up if I have to get in there."

"I wouldn't waste the food if I were you." He tries to smile.

"God, this is so not funny," I snap.

"I know that. Doesn't change anything. We're still stuck." He flaps his fingers for me to come on.

"Ten miles in this sludge."

"Seven maybe. Like I said, the levee is closer. Once we're there, it's dry land all the way to the highway."

Seven miles didn't seem that far. I walk to school all the time—a mile or so each way. *Who am I kidding?* I take a last look at the relative safety of the cabin, then at the gator. He's gone. Only a swath of small bubbles marks where he'd been. My breathing becomes shallow and rapid, and my heart thuds in my chest.

"I can't. I just can't," I say, but I close my eyes and am about to slip in when I hear a sound like someone slurping a Coke. My eyes snap open. "What was that?"

"A walking catfish."

There's a small splash as something leaves the surface. I hear the sound again and see a mouth in the water, or rather black lips around a hole in the water. Another surfaces, takes a gulp, and dives to the bottom.

"Are they eating? I've heard about fish that can spit a stream of water and knock a bug right out of the air."

I'm stalling. Maybe, if we wait just a few more minutes, we'll hear an airboat, or Andy will think of something else to try.

"They're breathing. Come on Sarah."

"They're fish, aren't they?"

"Yeah. Air-breathing fish." He flaps his hand again.

I close my eyes, say a little prayer, and tip forward off the dock.

7

The water was waist-deep on Andy, so I expect it to be chest-high on me. A scream catches in my throat as water pours over the tops of my boots. The added weight pulls me under and throws me off balance. I have a split second to gulp air like one of those catfish before landing on my hands and knees in mud that is up to my elbows. I try to swim out of my boots, but the angle is wrong. The harder I struggle, the deeper I sink until I'm on my belly, up to my armpits in the ooze with the boots clamped like vises around my ankles. Air leaves my mouth in a big brown bubble as I try to roll on my side. My eyes are open, but I can't see anything through the mud I've churned up. I pull an arm free and wave it above my head, hitting a dock post. Not a post; Andy's arm. I feel his hands around my wrist. He nearly pulls my arm out of its socket as he drags me upright. The water comes to my chin.

I gulp air and cough until my throat is raw. "What are you standing on?" I croak.

"The deck of the airboat." He leans and lifts me up into it with him.

My yellow T-shirt is slimy and brown. I cup my hands and bring water up to wash the mud off my face.

"I forgot you had those boots on. You can't walk in those." He puts his hands in my armpits and transfers me to the dock like a sack of potatoes. "You'll have to take 'em off."

"They are off. They're down there."

Andy gets on his knees, turns his head, puts his cheek against the water, and feels around until he finds first one then the other. He drags them up, rinses them out, and puts them the dock beside me.

"Now what?"

He sighs. "I'm not sure, but there's no way you can walk in those."

"We'll have to stay here and wait for help, I guess." My tone of voice is hopeful. I lean over to rinse my arms, then splash water on my shirt, trying to wash the mud off.

He makes a hiccup of a laugh and shakes his head. "That's the option we don't have."

Although the idea of nothing to protect my feet makes me sick, I point to the one of Andy's giant flip-flops that's now washed across the pond and is lodged between two cypress knees. "Could I wear those?" I look for the one I kicked off the dock. It's in the cattails that guard the channel into this place.

"You'd break an ankle for sure if you did. It's like walking across a coral reef out there—uneven, with dead trees and stuff hidden beneath the surface."

Beneath the surface. Those are the three scariest words in the English language to me right now.

"Once we're out of this pond, won't the water be shallow? Shallow enough to wear the boots without them filling up?"

"In a few places, maybe, but what about when it's not?" He slips his arms out of my backpack and puts it on the dock beside me. The bottom half is sopping wet; water gushes out through the zipper and drips from holes in the stitching.

"My Dad's binoculars and camera are in there."

"Well, they're done for now," he says flatly.

Please, not Dad's camera. I'm reaching for the pack when something in the water startles the duckling and it comes at us from near the propeller cage, its feet slapping the surface and wing nubs flapping.

I grab Andy's arm. "What's that?"

We both look toward the end of the pond where we last saw the gator. He's farther away, but still watching us with just his nose and bubble-shaped eyes above the surface.

"Maybe there's another one somewhere."

Andy looks at me like I'm an idiot. "I think you can count on seeing another one or two." He unzips the bottom section of the pack and takes out the camera and the binoculars. Water pours out of the binoculars, but the camera is all right in its baggie.

"Might as well leave these here."

Before I can stop him he pitches the binoculars toward the cabin. They disappear into the thick weeds. I grab the camera and hug it to my chest. "My dad will kill me if anything happens to this."

"I'll betcha it will never occur to him to ask what happened to either of them by the time he sees you again." Andy drives the blade of the butcher knife into the instep of one of my boots.

I grab the other one and hug it to my chest. "What are you doing?"

"Giving 'em drain holes." He twists the knife, trying to cut out a chunk, but the blade is too wide.

I feel around in the lower portion of the backpack and hand him my brother's Swiss Army knife. "This thing has scissors, I think."

There are a dozen blades and tools to choose from. "This really *is* a cool knife." He turns it over in his hand.

Andy first tries the little saw, then the scissors, neither of which can cut through the rubber. He finally chooses one of the smaller blades and finishes cutting two thumb-sized squares in the insteps. He dips the first boot and holds it up. Water gushes out the holes.

When he finishes the other boot, I pull them on. They are cold, clammy, and squishy inside. I step off the dock and stand beside him on the deck of the airboat. Water fills them again, and having the holes doesn't help at all. "This isn't going to work."

"Give 'em to me." Andy opens the saw-blade of the knife.

"What are you going to do with that?" I hitch myself onto the dock.

"You won't be able to put one foot in front of the other unless I get the water to run out as quickly as it comes in."

"Wait. Don't do that until we see if the water is over the tops when we get out of here."

"How are you going to get from here to there?"

"Swim."

He shrugs, then pulls himself out of the water to sit on the dock beside me. He takes off his tennis shoes and cuts holes in them, too. Before closing the knife, he stabs a small drain hole in the bottom of my backpack, puts the Spam in the lower half, the camera and the knife in the top half, and zips it closed.

It's been breezy for most of the morning, but it dies suddenly. A few minutes later, the sun disappears behind the southern wall of trees. Mosquitoes, which like shade and still air, appear instantly and seem to come to a boil around us.

I fan my face and squash them against my arms and legs, leaving bloody little streaks. "The bug spray's in the pack."

"You'll be in the water in a second."

"Please. I can't stand the sound of them."

"Spraying won't stop that." He puts my pack on again.

"Let's hurry then. Can I put my boots in the pack until we get out of here?"

He turns to let me unzip the bottom part. I stuff my boots inside and zip it as closed as it will go with the tops sticking out.

I slide off the dock and tread water like a frog with my legs splayed to keep from touching the bottom with my bare feet. I kick so hard that I don't sink above my waist.

Andy goes over the side of the boat and sinks to his armpits in the mud. Using his arms like water wings, he begins to plow through the water. I do the breaststroke so close behind him I keep bumping into his back. We've only gone a few yards when I slow and glance back to see if the gator has stayed put. It isn't there. My heart begins to ricochet inside my chest. "The gator's gone." Panic chokes off my breath. I swim around Andy and into the channel. The duckling, which has been swimming just off my right shoulder, peeps frantically and follows me.

I only get about a dozen feet ahead of him when my leg hits something hard and knobby. In a heart-stopping moment, I know it's the gator, yet I can't move. In my mind I see its pink throat and huge teeth coming up through the murky water.

Something brushes the back of my neck, and I scream. Andy has me by the collar of my shirt.

"There's a gator right there," I choke. "I touched it."

"If there is, it's dead. No gator in its right mind would just lie there." Andy feels around with his foot until he too hits the thing I ran into. He reaches down and feels it with his hands. "It's a tire off a swamp buggy."

"How would I know that?"

"Well, quit thinking everything is an alligator. They are more afraid of you than you are of them."

"Maybe that's true for you, but I can promise it's not so for me."

"Let's go." He starts off again.

The duckling's feeding on some pond scum. When I start to move, it skids toward me and nibbles at the tips of my hair, which is long enough to trail behind me in the water.

I want to think the pity I feel is for the duckling who's orphaned because of me, but it's myself I'm feeling sorry for. I'm glad it's with us. I'll have something to take care of, and I hope that will make me feel braver than I am. I reach to pet it, but it dodges my hand.

"You should leave that thing," Andy says. He's a few yards ahead of me. "It's slowing you down."

"It is not." I maneuver around the tire. "If you weren't racing ahead . . ."

"Racing? Get real. We have about six hours of daylight left. We need to get out of here and make some headway."

"I'll show you headway," I snap.

With the duckling following right behind my head, I swim past Andy and into the narrow, tree-guarded channel. I kick and splash, all the time imagining that fourteen-foot gator has sunk beneath the surface and is moving through the ebony water, gaining on me. My breathing is quick and panicky. I kick harder and don't stop until the tree canopy dissolves into blue sky.

Two hours ago, Andy had followed the thin, black remnant of a trail as it snaked through the cattails toward the cabin. Now, thank heavens, it feels wider because the airboat flattened the margins. I don't know what it is, but cattails, especially towering over me like they are, make me claustrophobic. I've never thought of myself as an easily frightened kind of person, but by the time I reach water shallow enough to feel the tops of plants brushing against my stomach, I'm gasping for air. I roll over on my back, looking for Andy.

He's where the trees give way to the cattails, in water to his thighs. "Try standing up," he says.

"Not without my boots." I float on my back, fanning my arms, and occasionally kicking to keep my feet from sinking to the bottom. Plants—at least I need to think they're plants and not water bugs or leeches or whatever's looking up at my back—tickle my arms and legs.

Andy catches up and sets my boots beside me.

I have to sit up to put them on. I let my butt settle to the bottom and find the surface is rocky and hard. I pull my boots on, then take Andy's hand and let him haul me to my feet. The tops of the boots end about six inches below my knees. The water level is two inches beneath the tops of my boots, but it doesn't matter since water seeps in through the holes he made and soon fills them to the same depth as the water I'm standing in. Instead of dry feet, they will be wet for however many miles this trek turns out to be. I force myself to smile. "Is it like this the rest of the way?"

"No," he says sharply, then adds in a softer tone, "but it won't be as bad as back there. They dynamited that pond out of the oolite."

"Oolite?"

"Limestone. It's what we're standing on."

I part the slimy brown algae to see the lumpy, sharp bottom. "It looks like coral."

"Yeah. It's old coral, I think—from another age. Just be careful walking. It's uneven and it's got holes in it."

"How come?"

"Don't know. Just does."

"But no more mud—like back there?"

"Only in gator holes, if we have to cross any."

This is the second time Andy's mentioned gator holes, and I remember Mr. Vickers talking about them on the bus, but I was too far back to hear what he said. "What is a gator hole?"

"A hole in the mud dug by a gator."

Andy seems to be lining himself up with something. He holds one arm up and looks at where its shadow falls, then turns a little to his left and glances at the sun.

"Why do they dig a hole?"

"So they have someplace to stay wet during winter dry-downs and warm during cold snaps."

Every time I ask Andy a question, the answer seems to make this place scarier—deep mud with a gator at the bottom. "Promise me we'll go around any gator holes, okay?" I twist my hair to wring out the water. I'd worn my hair down on purpose; now I wish I'd brought a scrunchie. It will dry frizzy, and I'll look like I'm wearing a rat's nest.

He doesn't answer. He's doing the arm thing again.

"What are you doing?"

"Nothing."

I guess he's getting tired of my questions, and I'm so happy to have made it this far and have my feet on something solid that I don't press him. There's a nice long stick floating nearby, and it occurs to me that it might come in handy, like a blind person's cane. I reach to pick it up. "Andy!" I fall backwards and scramble away, kicking water at it. The stick makes a quick turn and zigzags off through the saw grass. "That was a snake," I gasp.

"It was just a water snake. Probably after that damn duck." He puts his hand out to help me up.

My heart is still cart wheeling in my chest. "Stop, all right? I'm not leaving it."

"Sarah, you need to get a clue about what we're up against here," he shouts at me, gets control, and lowers his voice. "Worrying with that duckling is going to slow us down."

"Andy, I can't leave it behind."

"It's a mallard, for Christ's sake; they're as common as pigeons."

"It has nothing to do with how few or how many there are. Try to understand."

He throws his arms up in defeat, turns, and begins to walk.

He goes slowly, feeling ahead with his foot before taking a step. I do the same, which reminds me of the pink-footed wood stork we saw at Shark Valley. It, too, waded along shaking its feet, but to stir up food. *Food!* I wish I hadn't thought of that. We ate everything we had—except the Spam—and I'm starting to feel hungry again.

"There's a tree limb here," Andy says, stepping over it.

"Thanks." My calves already ache from lifting my heavy feet. I step over it and continue to shadow him silently, glancing back twice to see if the snake followed us. The duckling is paddling along beside my right knee.

"Andy . . ."

He stops and looks back.

"What kind of person would I be if I don't at least try and keep the duckling safe?"

"A sensible one." He squints thoughtfully. "I think you should let me snap its neck."

I stop. "You'd kill it? On purpose?"

"I kill our chickens all the time. It won't feel a thing."

"I don't believe you."

"What, that it won't feel a thing, or that I do it all the time?" He starts off again, leaving me to stare at his back.

He turns again. "You know what's wrong with bleeding hearts like you?"

"No, but I'm sure you're going to tell me."

"I live at the edge of a swamp. It's an hour's drive to the nearest grocery store. We raise chickens for food and for their eggs. They aren't pets. What you don't get is that people like me and my family care about what we can *afford* to care about."

"Did you think that up all by yourself?"

"Go to hell."

"You go to hell," I shout. "You're not touching her. I'll take care of her, and I'll take care of myself." I slosh past him, and the duckling peeps and swims after me. I've gone a couple of yards when I realize I don't hear him following me. I look back.

"It's this way," he says, pointing the opposite direction.

I turn around and the duckling follows.

8

This isn't so terrible.

We're out of the shadow of the tree-island and in the sun where the mosquitoes aren't bad, though it's broiling hot. My legs really ache because my boots have water in them to my ankles, which they wouldn't—I'm tempted to remind him—if Andy hadn't cut holes in them, and the tops are rubbing against the skin of my calves. That's beginning to hurt a little, too.

"Wait there," Andy says. He's been walking toward the skeletal remains of a tall tree, bleached to a pale gray. It has a number of branches left, pointing off in different directions. He glances at the sun and the cast of the tree's shadow. "That's east," he says—more to himself than to me.

"How do you know?"

He looks at me sharply as if he can't believe I'm that stupid. "Well, let's see." He scratches his head with his index finger. "Hum. It's probably about one, and the sun's headed that way, and since it usually sets in the west, that must be east." He points again. "But if you want we can stand here 'til it comes up tomorrow, just to make sure."

"Where do you get off acting as if I'm the idiot here?" I snap. "I don't see anything stupid about that question. And if you are so smart, what if it was noon? How could you tell which direction then?"

Andy deflates a bit but doesn't apologize; only his tone changes. "The days are getting shorter, so the sun is farther south. If we keep it off our right shoulders, we'll be walking east."

I'm actually impressed, but I'm not going to tell him. I watch him hang the Pan Am bag off an eastern-pointing branch and start back toward me. He's only gone a few steps when his left leg disappears and he falls over.

"Oh my God." I shuffle toward him.

He moans, closes his eyes, and doubles over.

My first thought is a gator has bitten his leg off, but I don't see any blood. He's definitely hurt badly enough that he can't answer.

"My leg," he finally groans. "Take the pack, please." He shrugs it off his shoulders and holds it out to me.

I reach, snatch it, and back away.

The duckling swims toward him.

"Come here." I pat my thigh.

The duckling does a U-turn.

Andy lies sideways in the shallow water for a full minute before he straightens, puts both hands against the bottom, and lifts himself up until he looks as if he's sitting on a bench just beneath the surface. I can see both knees.

"What happened?"

"I told you there were holes in the oolite. I fell through one. It was an uncomfortable landing."

It takes me a second to understand what he means. "Oh."

"Whoa," Andy yelps, and lurches backward. "Something just swam past my leg." He looks a little embarrassed by his reaction, grins, and holds his hand out to me. "Help me up, will ya?"

I put the backpack on, then slip my hands into his armpits and try to lift him. Once he's able to draw a leg out of the hole and get it on the hard surface, he lifts straight up.

"Did a gator make that hole?"

"No. Gator holes are big—some nearly the size of the pond at the cabin."

"You're bleeding." There was a tear in his jeans and a scraped, bloody piece of his leg showed.

"Not much I can do about it." He takes the backpack which, with the Gatorade, Spam, and Dad's camera, is pretty heavy. He shrugs it on.

"Does blood in the water draw gators like it does sharks?"

"No."

So he says, but I'm not sure he's sure.

. . .

We walk east for about thirty minutes in silence. I carry the duckling on my shoulder, cuddled against my neck with one hand over its back to keep it balanced until my arm starts to ache and tremble.

I watch every step I take, trying to see where to safely put each foot. Andy's just marching, getting farther and farther ahead. Every fifteen minutes or so he stops so I can catch up. We rest in open areas where the saw grass is short and sparse and lie back with our faces exposed to the afternoon sun. My arms and the backs of my bare legs feel sunburned and are raw where the boots rub against my skin.

It's such a relief to stop moving that the thought of having to get up and start again is almost more than I can stand. I try to guess the time and imagine, by now, Mr. Vickers has called my parents. My dad is usually a calm man who rarely raises his voice. He will try to think this through, list the possibilities and their options. My mother will be quietly frantic. My brother may be thinking about knocking out the wall between our rooms to create a suite for himself.

"What time do you think it is?" I ask. We're floating on our backs in the shallow water. The duckling is feeding on stuff near my right hip.

"Four-ish."

"I suppose my parents know by now."

"Probably."

"I feel awful."

Andy gets to his feet and holds his hand out to help me up. "I do, too, but there's nothing we can do about it."

I've started calling the duckling Teapot, because it reminds me of one—squat and pudgy, with a skinny little neck. Once I thought of it, the tune—*I'm a little teapot, short and stout*—plays in my head until I want to scream. *I'm losing it already.*

During one of our rest stops, Teapot swims over and waddles up on Andy's chest as he floats with his eyes closed. "Get your duck off me."

"She's not hurting you."

"I'm going to snap her neck," he says, but when I raise my head to look at him, he's stroking Teapot's back. "What makes you think it's a she anyway?" he asks.

I think about it for a minute, but can't think of a reason so I don't answer.

Andy lifts his dripping head and looks at me. "If one of them had to die, let it be a boy?"

"No." I sit up.

"What if they were both boys?"

"What difference does it make? Maybe I just want her to be a girl so we're two against one."

"I'm not sure getting out of here is a contest," he says, pushes Teapot off his stomach, and stands up. "Let's get moving." He holds his hand out to me.

I'm an athlete, but this is harder than any race. "Aren't you tired?" I say.

He shrugs.

"Walking in these boots is like having cement in my shoes."

"Are you planning to sleep here?"

I look around. "Where *are* we going to sleep?"

Andy points to a small stand of cypress, maybe a mile away.

"What's there? Another cabin?" I ask hopefully.

"No." He pulls me to my feet. "Just those trees."

"Then where are we sleeping?"

"In those trees—I hope."

"They don't look very big."

"Let's hope they're big enough."

"I'm hungry." My stomach is killing me.

"No food until we get there."

"Who died and left you in charge?"

He smiles for the first time since this morning. "If you were in charge, we'd be headed for Lake Okeechobee."

We slog on without talking. The sound of our splashing is comforting in a way.

He's waiting for me again. "Can't you go a little faster?" he says when I catch up.

Bite me, my mind snaps, but I just glare at him.

Straight ahead is a wall of cattails that stretches as far as I can see in either direction. The same irrational fear of them rises in me again, only worse this time. In the airboat we were able to see over them—see the other side and the way out. Once we're inside, it will be as if we've

84

been swallowed by green stalks. Still, when Andy starts through I follow, but the minute I feel surrounded, I stop. "Can't we go around instead? I don't like these things."

"What's not to like? They're plants."

"I don't know. They freak me out, that's all."

Andy shakes his head and comes back to where I'm waiting, hoping he'll say okay, we'll go around. "We have to keep going straight no matter what. If we start zigzagging around the hard parts, it will take us a week to get out."

"I'm so thirsty."

He turns to look at me. "How much water do you need?" He draws an arc with his hand.

"I can't drink swamp water. Animals poop in it, and there's all that slimy stuff floating around."

"Maybe we'll find a water fountain."

I stick my tongue out at him and immediately feel childish.

I've been shifting Teapot from shoulder to shoulder until both my arms ache from holding her in place. I lift the duckling off and put her in the water. All day I'd kept my bandana wet and draped around my neck. It's helped me stay cool, but the sun is getting low now and there is enough of a breeze that I feel a little chill. I knot the bandana around my neck, scoop Teapot up, and put her in the sling I've formed, then start forward again, trying to stay in the trail that Andy is opening through the cattails.

Two birds scream and lift off to my left. They startle me, but I swallow my cry. Small green frogs leap from the stalks into the water. The deeper into the cattails we move, the more impassably dense they become, and the bottom gets mushier. Mud has seeped into the holes in my boots, but I don't realize the water is getting deeper until it pours over the tops. I put all my effort into taking another step, but only the top half of my body moves. I fall over, twisting as I pitch forward so as not to crush Teapot.

Andy turns when I land with a grunt. "What happened?" He sighs heavily before coming back to help me up.

"These holes aren't working. My boots are full of water."

"That's 'cause more water pours in than can pour out two little holes. Take 'em off."

I don't want to stand barefoot in the mud, but I don't want to say so and have Andy roll his eyes, so I just lie there.

He figures it out, rolls his eyes, then bundles a dozen or more cattails together, twists them like fat, green strands of yarn, and folds them over. "Stand on these. That's the best I can do to keep your precious little feet from touching bottom."

"You think I'm a wuss don't you? Well, I'm not. I'm afraid of stepping on a snake."

"You are acting like a sissy. We're making enough noise to scare the piss out of everything in our path."

"I'm not acting like anything. I'm afraid of snakes and alligators. Anyone with half a brain would feel the same way. I'm not a backwoods redneck like you are."

Andy bites his bottom lip.

"I'm sorry." I squeeze my eyes shut. "I didn't mean that."

"It doesn't matter." He shakes his head. "Gimme your boots."

I sit on the pile of cattails and pull them off.

"What'd you do there?" Andy pointed to the raw, red marks in almost a complete circle around my calves.

"It's where the boots rub."

"Looks painful."

"Not too," I say. In truth, it hurts a lot, but I'm not going to complain about another thing. I'm too ashamed of what I called him. I, of all people, know what that feels like.

Andy pinches the top of a boot together and starts to make a cut.

"What are you doing?"

"They have to be short enough for the water in to equal the water out."

Using the butcher knife, Andy makes a long slit from the top to just above the ankles of both boots. He then tries to cut the tops off with the scissors, but they break apart without making a dent. My brother's face, as he hesitated to hand over his knife, pops into my mind.

I hold first one then the other by the bottom and the top while Andy uses the butcher knife to cut through until what remains are boots only as tall as my old hi-top Converse All-Stars.

"Now try 'em."

I pull on the cold, clammy remains and step off into the water. "Almost perfect," I lie. I take a couple of steps; they slap loosely against my anklebones, so loose that, if we get into any mud at all, I'll have to curl my toes to keep them on.

"They can't completely empty when you're in the water, but they should be a lot lighter."

"They are. Much." I touch his arm. "Thanks. And I really am sorry."

"It doesn't matter, Sarah. I am a redneck."

"I don't even know what that means."

"A hick. A bumpkin."

"I know the definition. I mean why *red* neck?"

He shrugs. "Who cares?"

"I do."

"Well, care later. Walk now."

The water gets deeper and the cattails denser, so dense that I have to elbow my way through the stand. The farther into them we get, the more suffocated I feel. The wet, soft strands of rotting cattails sliding across my bare legs make me feel like I'm wading through eels. My eyes snap from side to side, tracking every movement. I'm so consumed with watching what's happening around me that I run right into Andy, who's stopped suddenly. "What?" I peek around him.

We're at the edge of a clearing. There are maybe five yards of open water totally surrounded by cattails. For some reason, it makes me think of the eye of a hurricane.

That peaceful, quiet, sunny circle of blue sky, with killer winds whirling just beyond.

"*This* is a gator hole," he says. "Let me go first."

I almost laugh, but it couldn't have gotten past the lump of panic in my throat. "Okay," I whisper.

He doesn't even look at me or get that the suggestion that he might *not* be first in is funny. Andy begins by slapping the water and kicking his feet. For a moment there's no movement, then suddenly something huge and dark shoots out of the depths of the pond. Mud boils up as it plows through the cattails, flattening a trail as it goes.

I whirl around and try to break through the wall of cattails that have closed behind us, but a step or two in and I feel surrounded. I'm gasping for air. I spin and cover my mouth with my hands to keep a scream from escaping. I see Andy, with the backpack raised over his head, moving deeper and deeper into the black water until he has to tilt his head up to keep his nose and mouth above the surface. Just when I think he might have to go completely under, he begins to move up the far side.

"It will be over your head," he says when he turns.

He didn't see my panicky attempt to escape, so I try to act calm. "Okay," I say, but the quiver in my voice must have given me away.

"You all right?"

"Uh huh." I take Teapot out of the sling and put her in the water. The gator, which is about ten or eleven feet long, has turned and lies about ten yards away on a pad of flattened cattails, watching me. My heart bangs in my chest as I tuck my shirttail into my shorts and start across. When I'm in waist-deep, I slip off my boots and put them down the front of my shirt. With a final look at the gator, I swim across. Teapot, sensing my panic, passes me and skids to a stop beside Andy.

On the other side, I put my boots back on. "How come you didn't swim across?"

He shrugs. "Why swim when you can walk?"

We slog another few yards, then suddenly break out of the cattails and are back in a shallow saw-grass prairie. Andy flops down and lies back. "We can't rest long. It will be dark in a couple of hours." He closes his eyes. "You did great in there."

"Thanks." I lie with my head on his stomach. Teapot climbs onto my chest, shakes her stub of a tail to fling the water off, and nestles down. *We're like a little family.*

It seems as if only seconds pass before Andy pats my shoulder. "We'd better hit it."

I sit up. "I'm dying of thirst."

"Your lips are cracked. Don't you have lipstick or something?"

"In the pack."

Andy hands the pack over. I find my lip gloss in the top part, but am reminded by the weight of the bag, that there is Gatorade left. I take it out. "Can't we drink this?"

"You can have a sip or two, but we have to conserve it until I can find someplace to dig a scratch well."

"What's that?" I take a sip, hold it in my mouth, and play my tongue through it before swallowing. I hope it will make me feel as if I've had more. I hand the bottle to Andy.

"A scratch well is a well you dig in the mud."

"I don't think I want to drink anything from a mud hole."

"We'll see how thirsty you get."

"I'm pretty thirsty right now."

He takes about a teaspoon of the Gatorade, swishes it in his mouth, and hands the bottle back to me. "One more sip."

A different sound from anything I've heard until now gets his attention. He rotates his head like an owl trying to locate where it's coming from. Whatever it is sounds little, but while he's distracted, I take a big slug, screw the lid on, and put the bottle back in the pack.

Andy grabs my arm, puts his finger to his lips, and whispers, "Don't make a sound."

9

"What?" I whisper after a minute of not moving and barely breathing.

Andy's got his head cocked like a dog—listening. He puts his lips to my ear. "Didn't you hear that?"

"I heard a kind of peeping sound before." I listen for a moment; then, just as I shake my head, it starts again.

"That." He jabs a finger at the wall of cattails off to our left.

"It sounds like a puppy crying."

"Good description, wrong baby. There's an alligator's nest in there, and the babies are hatching. That sound is them calling to their mother to help them dig out of the mound." He looks left, right, and behind us. "There's nothing that will defend a nest like a mother alligator, and I don't want to get in her way."

"Let's go then."

"Keep your pants on. We could head off in the wrong direction and run right into her."

We stand where we are for a few minutes until—in the absolutely still air—I see the cattails begin to sway. "Here she comes," Andy whispers.

Just watching the cattails move gives me gooseflesh. There's no way to tell if she's headed toward us or to her nest which, judging from the little barking sound, is awfully close, but between us and her.

"Ouch." Andy pries my hand off his arm and shows me the half-moon dents my nails have made. "She's probably the co-owner of that gator hole."

"You mean she isn't the one who shot out of there?"

"Look for yourself." He nods to the right.

We'd created a gap in the cattails where we broke through. It's not a very wide break, just the width of us walking single file. From where we are I can see back down the trail we made, and I'm not seeing anything and say so.

"See those cattails moving?"

"Yeah."

"If it was a breeze, they'd be listing the same direction."

"Okay."

"Are they?"

"No . . ." They're being parted; something is coming along the trail we made.

"Do the fathers guard the nest, too? What if we're surrounded?"

"We're not surrounded. And the fathers could care less."

It's "couldn't care less," I think to myself, though I'm not at all sure why, under the circumstances, grammar has become a concern of mine.

The little barks increase, and we hear the scrape of the mother gator's claw against the mound.

"Come on," Andy says. "But no splashing. Pick your feet up."

Like that's easy.

We move straight out from the sound of the babies calling, then make a large, slow arc toward an old pond-apple tree on our left. It isn't very tall, but it's bushy, with thick sturdy limbs.

When we've put enough distance between us and the nest, we make a splashy dash for the tree. Andy climbs up first and pulls me up after him. The tree has lots of leaf-less, twiggy branches that cut and scratch my bare legs.

"There she is. Can you see her?"

I spot the volcano-shaped nest first. Leading away from it is a wide, muddy path of flattened cattails that opens to the water at the far end. The mother alligator is walking away from the nest and us, across the packed-down cat-tails. She reaches open water, glides in, and propels herself away with her massive tail sweeping back and forth like a thick wet noodle. "Where do you think she's going?"

Andy shrugs and starts to climb down.

"Wait. I want to see a baby hatch."

The mound is flat on top and reminds me of a swan's nest I saw once in a picture, only the gator's nest is bigger, a lot bigger, maybe seven feet across and three feet high. "How did she get all that stuff here?"

"I've never seen them do it, but a hunting buddy of Dad's watched one build a nest," he whispers. "It took days. She bites off the cattails and carries them here in her mouth. She even brings in branches and limbs and mouthfuls of mud. The mound heats up like a compost heap. I read somewhere that how hot it gets decides whether boy or girl gators are born."

"It's the same with sea turtles," I say and want to cry. "My dad . . ." Tears brim in my eyes. I swallow and start again. "When I was eight, Dad volunteered us with a sea turtle rescue group. Every Saturday that summer, he'd wake me before dawn and we'd drive to the beach at Crandon Park to dig up sea turtles' nests. The females come ashore at night to lay their eggs."

He glances at me. "How'd you find the nests?"

"We looked for the flattened mark in the sand the mother turtle's belly scraped as she dragged herself from her nest back to the water. We'd follow the trail, then dig up the eggs."

"Why bother?"

"Loggerheads are endangered. Moving the nest someplace safe gave the babies a better chance to survive. That's why we had to get there ahead of the beach-cleaning tractors, which drive up and down, scooping up the trash people left and the seaweed that washed ashore at high tide." I'm a little behind Andy in the tree, so he doesn't see the tears that slide down my face as I remember walking the beach, holding Dad's hand. "The eggs are shaped like ping pong-balls and rubbery..." I wipe my eyes with my T-shirt sleeve. "There were eighty or ninety, sometimes as many as a hundred. Dad would lift each one out like it was made of crystal, and I'd arrange them in a bucket. When we had all the eggs, he'd measure how deep the hole was, then we carried them to a fenced enclosure, dug a hole the same depth, and reburied them."

"When did they hatch?"

"In August. We'd get there before dawn each morning to check for hatchlings, and if we found a nest hatching we'd gather them up and carry them to the water. We got there one morning and found the gulls and frigate birds swooping on the babies that had hatched before dawn and crawled through the chain-link fence. It was awful. Dad gathered as many as he could carry rolled in the hem of his T-shirt, ran that load to the ocean, then came back for more. I ran back and forth waving my arms, screaming at the birds, and collecting as many as I could in our bucket."

I don't tell Andy, and I never told my dad, but I had nightmares for about a year after that. In them I was as little as a baby turtle and the birds were after me. Instead of hands I had tiny flippers that beat the sand as I made a mad dash for the ocean, where I imagined barracudas and eels were waiting to eat me. It never occurred to me before, but I bet that's why I'm afraid to swim in the ocean.

Right now, I feel like one of those baby turtles again. Here I am, making my way possibly to safety, or maybe just into deeper trouble. What did Andy know, really? Had he ever walked even a single mile in the Everglades? Why hadn't I asked him that before I traipsed after him? I look at the blue sky and the towering white thunderheads off in the distance, close my eyes, and wish with all my might that my father would appear and gather us up.

The mother alligator is returning. She lumbers out of the water and gently, with a front foot, scrapes away dirt and rotting cattails to expose a yellow-and-black striped baby. Another one wiggles out of the mound on its own. When there are four or five barking babies, she begins to eat them.

I grab Andy's arm. "Why is she doing that?"

"Shhh. Wait. She's moving them to a safer place."

The mother gator, with her jaws slightly open so her teeth form a cage, turns, trudges down her path, and slides into the water. She's gone only a minute or two when a great blue heron flies in, lands on the mound, spears a baby that has just emerged, bashes it to the ground a few times, then swallows it whole and flies away.

Andy whispers, "As my mother loves to say, what goes around comes around."

"Mine says the same thing," I say, but chill bumps rise on my arms. It's so life-and-death out here. Plain and simple. One minute you're fine, and the next you could be dead.

I'm still watching the nest when Andy starts to climb down. "Whoa," he says and steps back up beside me.

"What?" I look where he's looking. About ten yards away, at the break in the cattails, are two pigs—wild pigs, and one has tusks that arc up to form almost a complete circle. It's sniffing the air.

My own breathing turns to trembling gasps.

Andy puts his hand over my mouth. "Don't make a sound." He speaks against my ear. "They've got great hearing and a terrific sense of smell, but they can't see too good."

The boar is headed straight for our tree, sniffing, snuffling, and grunting. We can't climb higher, and his tusks look like they could cut us to ribbons.

From the nest, a baby gator calls. The boar stops. He listens for a moment, then turns left and sniffs the air again.

"This should be good," Andy whispers.

10

Since the hogs are too low to the ground to see the nest, which is beyond a barrier of cattails, they follow the sound, splashing toward it. We can see the mother gator coming back up her trail. She must hear them, because she stops, settles down on her stomach and waits.

Andy pries my hand off his arm again. "You've got quite a grip."

"Sorry."

The boar is in the lead when the pigs reach the mound. First he, then the female, put their heads down and start pushing into it with their noses. I nearly jump out of my skin when the mother gator hisses, rises up on all fours and charges. It takes just seconds for her to barrel the length of the trail, and only that long for the hogs to see her coming. The male grunts an alarm, and the two pigs run in different directions. The mother gator rips after the female. Her mouth opens and snaps closed. The pig squeals in pain, but escapes with just a gash in the flesh of a back leg.

We wait until the splashing and squealing stops, then climb down and start out again. The water is shallow and the view unobstructed, which gives my mind time to focus on all the reminders of how quickly a life can end.

. . .

"What time do you think it is?" I ask some time later.

"Six or six-thirty."

The trees we're headed for look more spindly the closer we get. "How far have we come?"

"Not far enough. A couple miles, maybe."

"Two miles! You're kidding?"

"Look back."

I turn and look where he's pointing. I can see the tops of some tall trees above the line of cattails we've just come through. "Those trees look sturdier, why don't we go there for the night?"

Andy laughs, then stares at me for a second. "You're joking, right?"

"I am not. That looks like a better place than where we're headed."

"Those are the trees around the cabin."

I'm leaning one way, then the other, trying to work out the ache in my shoulders. "You're lying."

"Why would I lie?"

"I don't know," I whisper. "I'm so tired. I thought we'd come much farther."

Andy walks over and puts an arm around me.

"I don't think I can go much further."

"You've got no choice, Sarah." His voice is soft. "You're doing great, you know? I'm proud of you."

"Are you?" I think about my dad and how he used to hug me when I was little. I feel that small and needy again, and the pressure of Andy's arms around me makes me cry all the harder.

"Hey. Come on." He kisses the top of my head. "A couple of miles are a good start. Think about it. At this rate, we'll do four or five miles tomorrow. Maybe the levee is closer than I think. Don't get bummed and start talking about giving up, okay?"

I nod against his chest.

He lets me go. "The bad news is, these trees ain't gonna work." His hands are on his hips as he looks at the thin, wispy branches of the cypresses.

"What can we do?"

He shrugs. "Keep walking."

"Andy, I can't take another step."

"You have to. We can't stay here."

"Once it's dark, how will we know that we're going the right way?"

"I'll worry about that then. Right now we've still got thirty minutes of dusk so we need to keep . . ." He stops and squints at the horizon. "Look."

"What?"

"Right there. See that light?"

My heart starts to race. "Is that a house or something?"

"No, it's the moon."

My heart sinks. Just breaking the horizon is an arc of golden light. Maybe I could manage another thirty minutes, but if the moon is up, he may want to keep going for hours. "We aren't going to try to walk by moonlight, are we?"

"Sure. It's full, or nearly so. We'll walk toward it until we reach the heron rookery. It can't be that much farther. I've been watching them flying in for a while now. See?" He points. Off to our right, a string of herons fly past— six, I count, then four more close behind.

"What's a rookery?"

"It's an island of trees where they come to roost for the night. Safety in numbers, you know. The roost is pretty near here."

"How far is pretty near?" I'm too tired even to slap mosquitoes.

In the dimming light, Andy shrugs. "It doesn't matter. We can't stay here, so the sooner we get started, the sooner we'll get there."

My legs have stiffened to boards. I struggle to lift a foot over a branch, trip and fall, cutting my knee on the sharp limestone. Andy doesn't stop, just calls, "You okay?" over his shoulder.

I'm too exhausted to answer. I get up and splash a little water on the cut on my knee to wash away the blood, then start after him.

My guess, from the position of the sun, is that we've been in the water for about five hours. All the energy I have left goes into putting one foot in front of the other.

. . .

Andy was right. Once the moon is up, it's bright enough to see our way, but a hundred times scarier. I keep his shirttail knotted in my fist.

During the day, the sounds were mostly startled birds and our own splashing, or the telltale *whoosh* of a gator rippling through the water. At night, all the sounds are strange. I'm less nervous when the frogs are croaking, but every once in a while something gets one. Its dying scream sounds like a woman's, and everything else hushes for a few minutes.

For the first hour or so after dark, we move through relatively open water with sparse, short stalks of saw grass. Animals run at our approach, then turn to look at us, red eyes glowing. With each new sound or pair of eyes, I cry, "What's that?" I'm not even aware that I'm doing it until Andy says, "Jesus, Sarah, give it a break."

For a while after that, when I ask, I try to sound calmer, and Andy obliges by naming the animal. He could be lying for all I know, but it helps to think he knows and isn't worried—or is at least pretending not to be.

We come to an area where nothing seems to be growing. Just a wide sheet of water dotted with a dozen small, round lights floating on the surface. Some are moving, rippling the water.

"What makes those little lights?" I try to sound relaxed.

"Gators. Their eyes glow when light hits them. That's why poachers look for them at night with flashlights."

"Why are they all together? What are they doing?"

"I don't know. Hunting, maybe. They're small."

"How can you tell?"

"By the distance between their eyes."

I'm not convinced and tighten my grip on his shirttail. I keep looking over my shoulder until it's clear they aren't coming after us. Still, every time my foot hits something in the water, my heart leaps and a little, lopped-off scream escapes.

It's easier to keep moving if I think of something besides how hard it is take each step. I begin to identify the sounds back to Andy. Knowing what things are doesn't stop them from scaring me nearly out of my skin. The easiest are the snorting, snuffling, and splashing of wild boar, then the throaty bellows and vibration of water made by male gators trying to attract a female. The sudden splashes of a deer leaping away with a flash of white tail in the moonlight is like having someone jump out at you from behind a door. Raccoons argue and screech at each other. Birds squawk and lift into the moonlit sky; then there's the occasional scream of a panther that makes the hair on my neck stand up. I've started to believe the gators *are* more afraid of us than we are of them, but I know a panther is different, and given a choice between me and Andy, it will pick me—the smaller, weaker one of the two.

There are moments, usually after the final cry of something dying, when the glades fall silent and there is only the sound of our labored breathing, soft moans when our feet hit something we have to step over, and the enduring sound of pushing through the weed-choked water. But when we stand still and rest, I can see that it's kind of pretty. The moon's reflection on the open patches of water is like a silver road to follow, and tree islands float like dark ships at sea. Off to the south a barred owl—the one bird I know by its call—hoots, and from the other direction another answers. I wonder if Mr. Vickers has ever seen it like this.

We've been walking long enough for the moon to shrink from an enormous orange ball on the horizon to its high-in-the-sky size when Andy stops suddenly, causing me to run into his back. "Smell that?" he says, sniffing the air.

I do. The breeze—which has kept the mosquitoes thinned—is out of the east and it carries the odor of bird poop—lots of bird poop.

"That's it," Andy whispers. "The rookery." He turns and puts a finger to his lips.

We move as quietly as we can, but the birds can see us coming. The moon is that bright, and it makes them more and more edgy. The closer we get to the stand of cypress and willows, the more restless they become. There's lots of wing-flapping, squawking, and pecking at each other. Some take off and circle, trying to find a better branch to settle on.

Andy's promise we would eat some of the dreaded Spam when we get to the roost makes my stomach start to rumble, and my legs get heavier in anticipation of stopping. Before swim meets, especially now that I'm on a scholarship, I sometimes have dreams like this where the more desperate I am to touch the wall, the heavier my arms and legs become, until it feels like I'm trying to swim through molasses.

I stop for a second to catch my breath and lean over with my hands on my knees. Teapot dangles in the sling around my neck. She's asleep, with her brown, yellow-cheeked head turned and tucked between her wings. I wonder for the millionth time today how I'd gotten myself into this mess.

Andy has stopped to wait for me. I cushion Teapot so she doesn't bounce against my chest, then straighten and start up again. I've taken two steps when my leg bumps a submerged tree trunk. I try to step over it but can't lift my foot high enough. I pitch forward, facedown with my arms out to break my fall. I feel Teapot struggling to get out from beneath me, but my arms are tangled in the branches of the tree and I can't get leverage to roll over. My head is underwater, so when I scream, the bubble of air breaks across my face.

I know better, but it's all I can do to keep from gasping for air beneath the surface. I fight and twist, trying to pull my arms free. Even underwater, I hear Andy crashing toward me then feel his hands in my armpits. He draws me, tree trunk and all, backwards so that I end up on my knees in the water with my arms still tangled in the dripping, slimy limbs. Teapot wiggles out of my bandana, drops into the water, and swims out of sight into some willows.

"Teapot," I cry. Then start to choke.

11

Andy snaps branches off until my arms are free, then pulls me to my feet. Blood seeps from a dozen cuts.

"Teapot!" I pat my thigh.

"You're welcome," Andy says.

"I'm sorry. Thank you. Just help me find her first." I look at him. "And don't say a word."

"Why would I waste my breath?" Andy puts a fist to his lips and makes a sound that is remarkably duck-like.

"Peep, peep," comes the answer from the weeds.

"Do it again." I stare at the black outline of the willows for movement.

Andy calls again, and Teapot swims out and straight into my cupped hands. I scoop her up and kiss her wet head. "That sound was cool." I smile at Andy. "Where'd you learn to do that?"

"From my dad. We hunt ducks, you know. We can't run to the supermarket for every little thing. Our meat comes on the hoof, not bloodless and wrapped in plastic."

"I get it already, okay. Why are you mad at me?"

"I'm not."

"You sound mad."

"Dragging that duckling along is making this harder than it needs to be."

"I thought we'd settled that. And besides, she hasn't bothered you all day, so don't start or I'll mention a few more times how we *got* in this nightmare in the first place." By the time I get to the end of the sentence, I'm shouting at him.

"Just shut up about that, okay? I know it's my fault." He stops. "Look, I'm sorry. I'm as tired as you are."

"It's okay."

"The closer we get to the trees, the more stumps and branches there will be. So watch out." He starts off again.

I'm trying to get Teapot to stay in the wet, cold sling. Andy has stopped and when I look up, he's watching me with his hands on his hips.

"Just go on, okay?" I say. "I'll catch up."

I'm so suddenly aware of myself and how exhausted, scratched, bruised, and bloody I am—it feels like part of me is floating on a string just above my own body. I can see myself standing knee-deep in a swamp the size of frigging Rhode Island or something. My hair is dripping wet. My skin stings from too much sun. I'm cold and shivering and wrestling with a baby duck.

"Why don't I put her in the top part of the backpack?" Andy says.

My out-of-body vision dies away. "Are you sure?"

He nods, then wades back and turns so I can unzip the top of the bag. My brother's Swiss Army knife is the only thing in there. I start to put it in the bottom half. "Hold her a minute, will you?"

"What are you doing?"

"I'm going to line the pack so she won't be sleeping in her own poop, and it will be easier to clean."

I cut a willow branch, strip the leaves off and coat the bottom of the pack. Andy hands Teapot over. I put her inside and zip it closed, leaving a pencil-sized gap for air to get in.

I see Andy smile. "What?"

"She ran back and forth a few times, then plopped down and peeped. At least one of us will get some sleep."

As we begin to move toward the rookery again, the birds closest to us grow more anxious. A few lift off, squawking, then land a little deeper in among the trees, dislodging somebody else, which starts another argument.

"Are we going to frighten them all away?"

"I don't think so," he whispers.

A few minutes later, a dark cloud moves across the face of the moon. The birds quiet.

"Let's go," Andy says. "This is our chance to get closer without them seeing us."

"But I can't see either."

"Take my hand."

I do and feel his calluses again, dry and rough. In the dark, his hand feels like my dad's. That comforts me.

We move as quickly as we can toward the trees, which are now a dark silhouette against the far-off, city-light glow of Miami and Ft. Lauderdale.

"Let's steer right until we find a tree big enough to hold us."

Turning right will take us to the south end of the tree island. Last night—*just last night? Is it possible?*—at the slide presentation, there was a series of aerial photographs showing the teardrop shape of most tree islands. Their shape, Mr. Vickers told us, was because water in the Everglades flows north to south, and debris, caught in that flow, accumulates at the north end. This build-up was future land where eventually shrubs and trees took root. The thickest tree growth was always at the north end where the soil had been collecting for the longest time. That's where most of the birds were, with only a few at the narrow south end.

"Andy, the largest trees are that direction." I point to the left. "I remember from the talk last night. That end is older."

"So?"

"Bigger trees have fatter branches. Shouldn't we go there?"

Andy stops. So do I. The cloud moves on, and everything's all silvery again.

"Well?" I say after a minute of just standing there.

"I'm thinking."

The closer we get to the trees and the birds, the worse the mosquitoes become. "While you're thinking, I'm getting eaten alive here."

"Okay."

"Okay, what?"

"We'll go to the north end." He turns left and starts walking.

"Andy."

"What now?"

"Shouldn't we walk up the east side?"

"What difference does it make?"

"Well, look at it. The trees block out the moonlight on this side."

Andy turns and trudges back toward me. When he passes, I follow, but I feel pretty smart to have figured that out and wish, at least, he'd noticed. "I'm tired, too, you know," I say to his back.

We stumble toward the south end, paralleling the hammock. When the trees end altogether, we make an arc around the tip of the island and start splashing and stumbling up the east side.

I've lost all sense of time, but it seems to take forever to reach the north end of the island. When we do get there, the grasses are also taller and denser. We have to cross through yards of tall saw grass to reach the trees. Andy goes first, holding his arms crossed in front of his face. I follow, but have taken only a few steps when I trip over a limb or a root, forget, and grab a clump of saw grass to break my fall. It feels like I've grabbed a fistful of needles. "Ouch."

"You okay?" He's reached the island.

"Yeah." My hand is sticky with blood. I rinse it and wipe it on my shirt.

"There's a huge strangler fig here." I hear him pat its trunk.

I come out of the grass, wind my way through some willows, and step up onto a tiny patch of dry land. Andy is in the tree, straddling a limb. He tilts his head back against the main trunk and closes his eyes. "Heaven," he says.

A large limb of the tree the fig strangled is broken off and lies like a nice wide ramp into the tree. I head for it, assuming that's how Andy got up there.

"Not that way," he says a second after I grab a small limb to pull myself up. It breaks away. Instantly I feel stinging bites on my hands, then my arms and legs and down into my boots. I scream and brush at the ants pouring over me. I scream again as they reach my neck and face. I can feel one in my ear.

"Get to the water!" He swings down from the tree.

I fight my way back through the willows and the dense saw grass to the open water, where I plunge in and roll like a gator.

Andy pulls me to my feet. "That limb was rotten." He drags me away from where I'd gone into the water, brushing my back. He digs his hands into the mud and smears it over my arms, then more over my legs. "Keep moving," he says. "They'll try to use you to crawl back out of the water."

My skin is on fire. Welts rise on my arms and legs.

We've frightened the closest birds, which have taken off and are circling, trying to land in a safer place.

"I lost one of my boots."

"We'll find it in the morning." He helps me rinse the mud off, then scoops me up, like Dad used to when I skinned a knee and cried, and carries me back to the hammock. At the base of the tree, he puts me down, then intertwines his fingers and turns his hands palms up. I put my bootless foot in the stirrup he's made and let him boost me onto the lowest branch.

The backpack is leaning against the tree trunk. Andy hands it up to me, then grabs a branch and, like a trapeze artist, swings his legs up and over an adjacent limb. "You okay?"

"My skin's on fire." I unzip the bottom compartment and feel around for the insect salve before I remember that I left it in my duffel bag. *How stupid was that?*

Teapot peeps sleepily.

Andy gets himself situated on a limb just above me while I spray my legs with insect repellent, which makes the ant bites sting worse. It's all I can do not to claw my skin. I hand the can to him and fan my legs. My one bare, crinkle-skinned foot glows white in the moonlight, except for my red toenails. They look as black as witch's lips in the dim light.

When he finishes spraying himself, he puts the can back in the pack and gets out the Gatorade.

"Just a sip or two, okay?" He hands it down to me.

I nod. The hunger headache that started hours ago is reaching migraine proportions from the ant bites. I sip the Gatorade, swallowing bitter-tasting bug spray with it. I run a finger across my lips. They are cracked and scaly. "Will you try to find my lip gloss?"

He reaches in and comes up with it and the Swiss Army knife. "Ready for dinner?"

We're seated on opposite limbs; his is a foot or two above mine. He breaks the key off the bottom of the can of Spam, then tilts it toward the moon to find where the metal zipper begins.

"How old is that stuff?"

"I don't know. Why?"

"I don't think cans open like that anymore. They open like dog-food cans with a ring you pull."

"It's not swollen or anything." He turns the key, and there's a *whoosh* as air enters the can and the smell of Spam escapes. He sniffs it and smiles. His teeth are as white and even as pearls in the moonlight. Mine feel as scummy as a mossy rock.

In spite of how disgusting the thought of eating Spam is, my stomach growls loudly.

"I guess you don't want any, right? I think I remember you saying you wouldn't touch this stuff if you were starving, or was it if your life depended on it?"

I look up from clawing at my ant bites. "The time for jokes was about seven hours ago."

"Don't scratch. It'll just make them worse," Andy says.

"I can't help it, they're driving me crazy."

With the can balanced on his knee, he cuts the meat into two remarkably equal chunks. He hands me one of them.

I sniff it, then tear half off with my teeth, chew it a couple times, and swallow with a shudder.

"Don't eat it all . . ." his voice trails off. "At once."

I break the rest into smaller bites, then swallow each like a pill with a slug of Gatorade. I'm not too crazy about Gatorade, but it does help wash the taste of Spam away.

"Save a little for me," Andy says.

I hand him the bottle. "All yours."

"You'll be sorry. That's all we have." He cuts his Spam into two equal parts, then cuts those two pieces each in half. He puts one quarter in his mouth and chews and chews and chews.

I want to slap him.

One of the quarters he puts in the pocket of his shirt. "Breakfast." He smiles. He drops the other two pieces, one at a time, back into the can. "Lunch." *Thunk.* "Dinner." *Thunk.*

From where I'm sitting, I could easily grab his ankles, lift and tip him off his perch, and happily watch him fall right on his smart ass.

He takes two short sips of Gatorade, then puts everything back in the bottom of the backpack. "You should have saved some for tomorrow. Don't ask for any of mine."

"Wouldn't think of it." It had almost made me gag to eat it at all. Even the food we feed the stray dog we've adopted looks more appetizing than Spam, and it comes with gravy.

"I don't think I can sleep like this." The branch I'm on is thick enough to straddle, but I feel tippy when I lean back against the trunk. A breeze blows across my legs, which helps with the mosquitoes and cools the ant bites, but makes me shiver.

"You may not sleep, but I plan to." Andy reaches up and hangs the backpack on the branch above his head. "If a bear comes, he'll have to crawl over me to get my Spam."

"Jesus, there are bears out here, too?"

"Sure. Spam-loving black bears."

"I bet the smell alone will draw them from miles around." I mean it as a joke—kind of.

Andy doesn't answer, and I wish I hadn't thought of the possibility and another reason to be scared.

I change position to sit crosswise on the limb with my arm around the main trunk, but the bark presses uncomfortably into my goose-pimply, ant-bitten legs. I untie Dad's shirt from around my waist, drape it over my knees, and tuck the sleeves under my thighs where the branch presses into my skin.

A cloud had drifted across the moon, but now it moves on, exposing dozens of nervous birds scattered throughout the trees behind us. Not just great blue herons, but brilliantly white common egrets in the canopy, the smaller snowy egrets and white ibises beneath them. They look like ghosts among the black, leafy branches. Except for the mosquitoes whining, the distant but ominous rumble of thunder, and the discomfort of tree bark pressing into the welts on my skin, there is something about being with all these birds that is comforting. They make me feel safer.

My face is swollen and sore and it hurts when I put my cheek against the tree's bark. I touch my skin. It's as lumpy as a toad's. I pluck twigs and pieces of grass from my hair, then twist a wad of it into a bun and place it between my ear and the tree trunk. I close my eyes. They sting, too.

"Remember what you said about what goes around, comes around?" I say.

"Yeah."

"Do you believe that?"

"I guess, why?"

"Do you think this is our punishment?"

"Yours maybe."

"Why not yours?"

"I'm not the one who lied to my teacher and snuck off with a boy I hardly know."

"Very funny. You *are* the one who forgot the stern plug."

Andy doesn't say anything.

"Are you asleep?" I ask after a few minutes.

"No."

"Will you hold my hand?"

Andy groans, then tries to reposition himself, but only the tips of our fingers touch. "I can't reach you."

His right foot is close enough to smell of swamp. I untie his shoelace and loop a few inches around my little finger, then close my eyes and hope it's too dark for him to see how lumpy and ugly my face is.

Only seconds pass before we hear splashing a few yards away. "What's that?"

"Wild hog, probably."

"What would you give for some bacon right now, or a ham sandwich or ham and macaroni and cheese?" My stomach feels like there's a bubble of nothing but air in it.

"Talking about food only makes it worse."

I shift again and finally angle myself so when I lean back another limb hits me across the back of my neck. It's miserably uncomfortable, but at least I'm not afraid that if I manage to doze off, I'll fall out of the tree.

Thunder rumbles—closer this time. Teapot peeps in her comfy, warm backpack. What I'd give to be able to shrink down small enough to fit in there with her.

It's getting cloudier. Now and then the moon is blotted out, and the birds quiet down. Even the frogs fall silent. I get a picture in my head of Teapot and Andy and the birds all slipping away while the moon is hidden and leaving me here alone.

"Do you have brothers or sisters?" I say.

"No. You?"

"A brother. He's two years older."

We must have been hanging in the tree for about an hour when the first raindrop hits. It's big and fat, which means a downpour. I open my eyes in time to see a flash of lightning that turns the landscape into a negative—the sky white and the trees and the prairie black.

I cry out. I can't help it. "We can't stay in this tree if there's lightning."

"Where would you feel safer? In the water?"

"No, but maybe we should get down until it's over."

"Go ahead."

Andy has found two branches that grow nearly side by side. He's crossed his legs at the ankles, and they are propped up on a limb that is higher than his butt. His back is against another branch so it looks like he's sitting in a comfortable lounge chair.

The top of the towering storm cloud looks rimmed in silver with the bright moon behind it. I wait for another flash of lightning to look for someplace safer; a clearing in the bushes where I could crouch to wait out the storm. When it comes, it's followed by a crash of thunder that startles me so badly I almost lose my balance.

I hear the backpack zipper. "What are you doing?"

"Getting the Gatorade bottle."

"To catch some rain?"

"Yeah."

A moment later the sky opens up and the rain comes down with such force that it feels like BBs. I sit up, wrap one arm around the main trunk, and lean over, leaving only my back exposed to the bruising rain. Just when I think I couldn't possibly be more cold and miserable, a gusty wind kicks up.

"Are you awake?" I say.

"Of course."

"I'm freezing." My teeth chatter.

"If you hadn't worn shorts . . ."

"If I'd known I'd be walking home, I wouldn't have. Just remember who got us into this mess."

"Yeah, well, you remember who's doing his best to get us out of it."

I hate you.

DAY THREE

12

As soon as the rain stops, the mosquitoes return. I have Dad's shirt over my back, but now it's sopping wet so they can bite right through. The cold has made my leg muscles knot up, and my skin feels stretched so tight over the swollen ant stings that a mosquito bite might pop me like a balloon. I need the bug spray.

"Andy," I whisper.

He doesn't answer. I can't believe he's actually asleep, but just in case, I rub my legs, then work them back and forth, trying to defrost my muscles. I encircle the tree trunk with my arms and shinny up until I get my feet under me. Once I'm standing on the limb, I can reach the backpack and manage to unzip the bottom portion, but I'm shivering so that I fumble the can of spray and drop it. It lands with a hollow metallic ping at the base of the tree.

I've seen crazy people in movies, and I know I must already look the part, my hair wild and full of twigs, saw grass, and drying bits of algae. I want to scream, but if I do, I'm not sure I can stop.

Teapot peeps sleepily; that little sound brings me back.

"Andy."

"Yeah?"

"I dropped the bug spray."

The moon is out again. By its light I watch him straighten his legs and rub them, trying to get the circulation going. After a minute or so, he grabs a branch, swings down, and drops to the ground. I watch him look around for the dark green can.

"It landed right below me." My voice is shaking. I'm being eaten alive. "Did you find it?" *Find* comes out shrilly.

Pssst. He's spraying himself.

"Do my back and my legs, will you?"

He doesn't answer, but in a moment I feel the burn of the stinky spray on the ant bites. When he finishes he hands me the can. Without a word, he climbs past me and settles back into his lounge-chair position.

I spray myself, face to feet, then cautiously jam the can into the crotch of the tree just below me. "Thank you."

"You're welcome."

"Did you catch much water?"

"A little."

"Can I have some?"

He reaches into the open pack and hands down the Gatorade bottle.

"Don't let Dad's camera fall out."

"I won't."

I hold the bottle up to the light. It's not a very big bottle, and it's only about half full, which, as I recall, was about what we had before the rainstorm. "'A little' is an overstatement," I say, then glance up at him. I wonder if he drank some when I wasn't looking, but I don't ask.

. . .

There's no way to tell how much time passes; long enough for the numbness in my legs to set in again. Some time later, Andy starts to snore, which makes me feel totally deserted.

Now that the storm is over, the glades are full of noise once more. By the brightness of the moon, birds scold and bat each other with their wings, jockeying for position. Each species of frog has its own distinct croak. I can recognize bullfrogs and pig frogs, which grunt like miniature hogs, and the little tree frogs, whose call has a higher pitch. They all stop when something screams. From somewhere in the shadows, I hear a low rumbling kind of growl.

"Panther," Andy whispers.

"How close?"

"Not too."

Hours pass before I finally doze off. If my hand hadn't slipped off my lap and whacked a branch, I wouldn't believe I'd slept at all. A little later, the mosquitoes begin to bite again. I carefully pry the can out of the crotch in the tree and apply a fresh coat. The can feels depressingly lighter. It's Sunday. If we don't get out until Tuesday, it won't last. Not with both of us using it.

The next thing I know, something's burning my left shoulder. I open my eyes. The sun. I try to move, but every inch of me hurts. I glance up to see if Andy is awake. He isn't there. I sit up with a start and look around. He's gone, and so are all the birds. "Andy!" I scream.

From the backpack comes frantic peeping and the sound of toenails on canvas.

"Andy?" I'm trying not to panic. What will I do if he's left me? How long has he been gone? Long enough to break a leg, be bitten by a snake, or killed and eaten by an alligator. Should I try to find him or stay here? Maybe he's gone on ahead without me slowing him down, and will send help back for me. He should have told me what he was going to do.

What's that? I hold my breath and listen. *Splashing.* Something in the water coming closer. "Andy?"

"Morning."

"Where were you?"

"Answering nature's call."

"Huh? Oh. Where are all the birds?"

"They left at dawn."

"I guess I really did fall asleep."

"Snored like a lumberjack."

"I did not." I unhook the backpack and hand it down to him. "Someone wants out."

Andy, holding the pack above his head, walks out the path through the willows and grass to the water. When he unzips the top, Teapot leaps out and swims in ecstatic little circles, flapping her stubby wings. She drinks by dipping her beak and lifting her head, then starts to hunt for food, slurping up floating bits of green stuff and poking her head below the surface, her little downy brown butt in the air. Andy and I watch her for a minute, then look at each other and smile.

I slept with my remaining boot on, figuring it would be easier to find one lost boot than two. The rain poured in the top and out the holes, leaving only a puddle in the heel, but in the humid air the entire inside stayed wet all night. Both my feet itch like crazy. Though the bootless one is dry, it's hugely swollen from the ant bites.

I lean and pull off the wet boot. "Oh my God, look at my foot." It's wrinkled and white, like skin under a wet Band-Aid, except for my bright red toenails. The heels and the balls of both feet are raw where blisters formed, then popped. The skin around my anklebones, where the boot tops rubbed, is also inflamed.

Andy looks up from cleaning out the top of the backpack and makes a face. "Bet that hurts?"

"Of course it hurts." Snapping at him drains me. "Every inch of me hurts. I can't tell where my feet leave off and the rest of me starts."

I touch my face, and the feel of the bumpy mosquito and ant bites reminds me of how awful I must look. I can't get my fingers through my snarled, gummy hair. For a second, I almost wish Andy had gone ahead for help rather than see me looking like some swamp creature.

"Did you find my other boot?"

"Look down."

It's at the base of the tree. "Thanks."

Andy comes forward and holds up his arms. I put my swollen hands on his shoulders and tip off my perch. When he lowers me to the ground, raw pain shoots up both legs. I squeeze my eyes shut and groan.

"You okay?"

"How am I going to walk today? My skin's rotting off."

"That's stretching it a bit, but I'll give you my socks to wear."

I hear "stretching it" and open my mouth to remind him none of this is my fault, when the "socks to wear" sinks in. "You will?"

"I can also cut notches in the rubber for your anklebones."

"Where's Teapot?" I look around.

Andy gives a short duck call, and Teapot swims at us from a patch of saw grass. About three feet behind her is a water moccasin. Before I can even scream, Andy hits the snake with the backpack. Teapot flees into the willows.

In a single motion, Andy leaps forward, catches the stunned snake by its tail, and throws it like a boomerang, so quickly I see the snake's cotton-white mouth snap shut in the air near its own tail while it's still airborne.

Andy looks at me and puts his finger to his lips. That's when I realize I'm screaming uncontrollably—short, gasping screams.

"Shhhh," he says. "It's gone." He calls to Teapot again, and when she waddles toward him, he scoops her up and hands her to me. "See. She's okay."

I press my cheek against her. "I just want to go home." With my back against the tree trunk I slide to the ground and cry until I give myself the hiccups.

While I'm sobbing like a baby, Andy just stands there staring east, his hand up to shield his eyes against the morning sun. "Maybe we'll make the levee today," he says. When the hiccups start, he squats beside me and tries to smooth my hair.

"Did you break . . . *hic*. . . Daddy's camera?"

"It's fine."

I lean against him with Teapot cradled in the crook of my arm. I think of the others girls just waking in the cabin, or have they cancelled the rest of the field trips? Are they all on the bus headed back to Miami? What are my parents doing? I've never spent a night away from home, except with them on vacations. And poor Mr.

Vickers. What must he be going through? *I'm all right,* I think as hard as I can, trying to send a mental message across the miles.

Andy and I hold on to each other for a few more minutes before I take a deep breath and wipe my eyes with the sleeve of Dad's shirt. "Okay," I say. "I'm ready."

Andy kisses the top of my frizzy head, stands, and helps me up.

With his hand against the tree trunk, he takes off his sneakers, then his socks, and hands them to me. "Put these on while I work on your boots."

Using the saw, he tries to cut semi-circles for my anklebones.

His socks are cold and wet. After the initial shock of pulling them on, they feel good against my burning, itchy feet. "What about the scissors?"

"Broke those yesterday, remember?"

He finally manages to saw a vee into both sides of each boot.

"Is that better?" he asks when I have them on.

"Much," I lie. With the socks on my swollen feet, the boots are snug—uncomfortably so—like shoes a size too small, but if my choice is between more blisters or cramps in my toes, I'll take cramps.

With Teapot stowed in the top of the pack, we start out.

"Watch out," Andy says, and points to a clear patch of water.

It's where I rolled to wash the ants off, mashing down all the vegetation, but after the moccasin, my heart leaps. "What?"

"See your ants?"

I stop. Floating on the surface is a small writhing circle of red ants—the living ones on a raft of dead bodies. I walk back to the willows and break off a branch.

"What are you doing?"

"Giving them a bridge."

"You're kidding," Andy says.

"No. I'm not." I lay the branch down so the ants have a way to get home. "I keep thinking about what you said, 'what goes around comes around.' I want to do all the right things out here, Andy, just in case it's true."

. . .

We haven't gone a hundred yards when I smell pumpkin bread frying. The smell is so strong, my mouth waters and my stomach growls. "Do you smell that?"

"Smell what?"

"Never mind." No sense making his stomach hurt too by mentioning what I'm only imagining.

For the first couple of hours, I feel light-headed. My stomach aches and my mouth feels stuffed with cotton. "Could I have just a tiny sip of the Gatorade?"

"Not yet."

"What are we waiting for?"

He doesn't answer.

The walk itself is like it was yesterday, except that I'm hungrier and each step hurts my feet and my leg muscles are cramping. A moaning little aaahhhh comes out with each step I take.

I know from swimming that the strain of this much exercise is depleting the oxygen in my muscles. For a while, I try blowing through pursed lips, like I've seen women who are having babies do on TV, but that just gives me another thing to have to remember: puff air, look out for snakes, and watch where I'm stepping.

Before we left the hammock, Andy broke off two pretty sturdy limbs for us to use as walking sticks, but it only helps a little. A couple of times my legs stop moving. I just stand quietly and watch Andy walk on. I can't wrap my mind around taking the next step. If he goes, or if he stays, is meaningless to me.

But he does stay. "What's wrong?" he turns and asks.

"Nothing." Then I put a foot forward and start moving again.

Things in our path slither away in startling bursts of speed. If what flees is a gator, it leaves a trail of tiny bubbles on the surface. Turtles dive beneath the mats of algae. Frogs swim to the bottom, then float back to the surface. Fish—mostly gar—zip away with a departing splash from their tails. Water snakes, once they sense the vibration of our approach, swim away along the surface and disappear into the saw grass.

By the height of the sun, I guess it's about noon when we come to a hammock straight out of the slide show of two nights ago. It has palmettos and sable palms and beautiful gumbo limbo trees, "tourist trees," Mr. Vickers called them because the red trunks look sunburned and bits of the bark peel off in pale, thin strips. It's a long island, and too dense just to barrel through. We stand side by side and look left, then right.

"How wide do you think it is?" I ask.

"I don't know, but I can't see daylight through it."

"Me either."

Andy looks at me. "We need to keep going east."

"I know, but I don't think we should try to go through it." I let Teapot out for a swim and to feed. "What if we try and it's really thick and wide? We could end up going in circles."

Andy doesn't say anything.

I want no part of bushwhacking through the dense growth. Moccasins are one thing. At least we can see them coming in the water. Rattlesnakes are another. Unless we come across one that is feeling generous enough to sound a warning, it would be hidden right up until the moment it bit one of us.

"It will take a lot longer, too. We'll have to cut our way through with nothing but that butcher knife," I add.

Andy just stands there like he's in a trance or something.

I touch his arm. "The trail is south, so by walking south aren't we going the same direction we'd be walking on the levee?"

"I guess," he says.

"As soon as we get around the south end we can turn east again." There's something in Andy's expression that worries me. "What's wrong?"

"Nothing. I just have a massive headache."

"You're hungry. Where's your stockpile of Spam?"

"I ate it this morning."

"Well, drink some Gatorade."

Andy's eyes don't meet mine.

A shock runs through me. "Did you drink it all?"

"I'm sorry."

13

"How could you?" My voice comes out raw and croaky. Now that there is nothing to drink, I feel my throat close with incredible thirst.

"I'm bigger than you are."

"That's bull!" I shout, even though I do remember the extra gulp I took yesterday. I didn't drink it all.

"I'm sorry. I only meant to take a sip, but when I did I couldn't stop."

"You said when we got to a tree island you'd dig a scratch well. Here we are."

Andy looks at his feet. "I'm not really sure what it is. My dad once told me it was a way to get clean water, but I've never needed any."

"Well, we need it now, don't we?" I can't cover how mad I am. If I'd been in charge of the diluted Gatorade,

I'm pretty damn sure I wouldn't have drunk it all. I'm scared and hungry, thirsty, and in pain, too, but the worse I feel, the more determined I am not to sink to some depraved level where my needs take priority over Andy's. I trusted him to feel the same.

Andy stands staring at the tree island in a kind of stupor. "I guess you just dig a hole in the ground and let it fill with water," he finally says.

"The only dry ground around here is in that hammock, so let's try it." I pat my thigh for Teapot, put her in the backpack, and start for the trees.

Like the hammock we came from, this one too is protected by dense saw grass, then a line of willows. Andy goes first, with his hands up to protect his face. I follow, but when we get ashore the plants are growing so densely there's no bare ground. We wade back out and parallel the shore for a dozen or so yards until we see a real trail to the island.

I start up it, but Andy stops.

"What?"

"Want to guess what made this?"

It's wide, and all the long grasses have been flattened just like the trail to the gator's nest. "Oh." I come back and stand beside him. "Another mother gator?"

Andy shrugs, but slips the butcher knife out of his belt and starts up, splashing noisily. Teapot's head pokes out of the backpack and rotates like a periscope. In spite of myself, I giggle. Andy—great white hunter and his faithful duck scout.

"Teapot's got your back," I tell him.

"Huh?"

"Nothing."

The trail is about twenty yards long and curves to the left before it opens up flat and wide like a spatula. It's not until we make the turn that we see the gator lying on the bank in the sun. Its mouth is closed and its eyes are on us. It's small compared to the one at the cabin, but still seven or eight feet long.

"Let's go," I whisper, and began to back away.

Andy doesn't move. "Go right," he says after a moment, jerking his head toward the edge of the island farthest from the gator.

"I don't think this is a good idea," I say. "What if it charges us like that mother did after the hogs? Mr. Vickers said they can run thirty-five miles an hour."

"They can, but only for a short distance."

"Exactly how far is a short distance?"

Andy shrugs, then, still facing the gator, catches my hand and steps sideways, pulling me with him.

Walking across the flattened grasses was pretty easy, but to get to dry ground we have to wade through soupy black muck. Even wearing Andy's socks I have to curl my toes to keep my boots on. Had the socks been clean and dry, they probably would have reached my knees. Instead, they form bulky, muddy clumps around my ankles. After a yard or two I drop Andy's hand, lean and pull a foot free, take a step, reach and pull the other one free to move a single pace. I keep this up until we reach the shore, where I drop to my knees, crumple to the ground, and roll on my back. My breathing comes in short gasps.

"There must have been a camp here once." Andy sinks to his knees beside me.

"Why do you think that?" My breathing slows.

"This is St. Augustine grass—like for a lawn," he says. "Someone had to have brought it here."

I raise my head to look at the gator, estimating the distance between us to be only about ten yards. It has closed its eyes, but there is something else moving through the grasses near the trail.

I sit up and shade my eyes against the sunlight. Whatever it is slides slowly along beneath the flattened grasses, creating a hump like a mole's trail. "There's another . . . Andy!" I grab his arm. My cry startles the gator, but it's too late. Like a flash of lightning, a giant snake strikes the side of the gator's face.

"Holy Christ." Andy jumps up and jerks me to my feet.

I bite my fist to keep from screaming. Blood whooshes in my ears. Minutes ago, Andy and I walked right past that snake.

The gator tries to pull free by whipping its tail from side to side. The snake is massive, as long as twenty feet, and must weigh close to two hundred pounds. It has brown patches outlined in yellow, which make it look like an ugly, rolled-up quilt.

Each time the gator moves the snake arches its neck, trying to roll it over on its back. They thrash for a few minutes, then lie still.

I'm shaking so hard Andy puts his arms around me to hold me in place. "What kind of snake is that?"

"A Burmese python. I've heard they're out here, but I've never seen one." His voice trembles, too.

"How... how did they get here from Burma?" I stutter.

"People buy little twenty-inch babies as pets. When they grow big enough to start eating members of the family, they get dumped out here."

"You mean there are more of them? How many more?"

"Who knows. Dozens. Hundreds. It's anybody's guess."

"Good God, Andy. That could be one of us."

The python and the alligator are locked together, neither moving. Mr. Vickers talked about how easy it is to hold the jaws of an alligator closed. "With one hand," he'd said. "They have strong muscles to snap shut on prey, but weak muscles to open their mouths." The snake got the gator mid-jaw so it couldn't bite back.

My legs tremble. I can't hold them still, and I can't take my eyes off the pair of reptiles. The snake is trying to work the tip of its tail under the alligator's stomach. A ten or more foot section of the snake lies in a loop across the grass for balance against the gator's attempts to pull free. "Shouldn't we get out of here while we can?"

"It could take 'em hours to end this," Andy says. "We need water." He gets on his hands and knees and begins to dig.

I glance down at him as he claws the ground. "You kept the bottle, didn't you?"

"Of course."

I squat down, unzip the top of the backpack to free Teapot, then take out the empty plastic bottle and put it beside Andy.

His fingers blacken. "I'm really sorry, Sarah," he says without looking at me. "I just lost it this morning. I was so hungry and thirsty I couldn't think straight."

"Let it go, okay? It doesn't matter anymore."

It's nearly impossible to take my eyes off the life-and-death struggle going on just yards away, but when I glance to check Andy's progress, I realize drinking all the Gatorade does matter. Death for that alligator, assuming the snake wins, will have come without warning. Andy and I are in a life-or-death situation of our own, but up 'til now I've blindly put all my trust in him. He groans with the effort he's putting into digging, and I understand if this doesn't work, we'll have to drink the swamp water. If it makes us so sick we can't go on, or only I get sick, but something happens and Andy doesn't make the levee, we're goners. The Gatorade matters because it was never fair to expect him to carry responsibility for himself and for me.

He straightens and pushes his hair off his forehead, smearing it with mud. Sweat stains the back of his T-shirt like it did my dad's when we were side by side on our knees digging up turtle nests. Pain spreads through my chest at the thought there's a real chance I'll never see either of my parents again. A picture of them in the bleachers watching my first swimming practice comes to mind. They sit close together, holding hands, but apart from the few other parents who are there. I was embarrassed because they were beaming at me like a pair of Cheshire cats. All I could think of was how I'd never wanted to go to Glades Academy in the first place. I understood why it was so important to them that I got in, but my friends and my brother were at Tucker. I look at the empty Gatorade container, then at the two reptiles. All Mom and Dad want is for me to have a better life than theirs. Whether I succeed or fail at that is up to me. I put my hand on Andy's shoulder. "Move over."

The soil feels moist and lumpy, like cookie dough. I dig harder as water seeps into the cavity. I glance at the snake and the gator, then sit back on my haunches to watch as muddy water oozes into the hole.

"The water's filthy," Andy says.

"We need something to dig deeper with." I look around.

"Why? What good will it do? We can't drink that."

"Find something to dig with. A stick or something."

Andy studies the woods, and I see a light go on in his mind. He roots in my pack for the knife and opens blades until he finds the saw. He crosses the narrow clearing to a palmetto and pulls off one of the fronds. He uses the saw to cut the leaf-head off. When he comes back, he's shaped the end that had been attached to the trunk of the palmetto into a pretty serviceable shovel.

"How's this?"

I straighten and rotate my aching shoulders. "Perfect."

"I've got a little present for you." He brings the leaf-head from behind his back. He's cut and shaped a handle, then trimmed the fan-shaped leaf down until it is just the right size. "Maybe this will help with the mosquitoes." He hands the fan to me.

"Thanks."

"I really am sorry."

I pat his dirty, sweaty arm. "It's okay, really. I never much liked Gatorade anyway, and it tasted worse diluted."

While he digs, I fan us, scattering the mosquitoes. The python and the gator are motionless, just their sides heave. I lie back on the grass and stare up through the branches of a gumbo limbo tree. A breeze moves the tops, but where we are, the vegetation is too thick to feel any wind. The sunlight flickers across Andy's back.

It feels so good to be lying down, off my stinging, burning feet, that I close my eyes, but after only a moment I imagine the python has given up on the gator and is sliding toward us. I gasp and sit up.

Andy looks at me. "What?"

The snake and the gator haven't moved.

"Nothing."

The hole is wider and deeper, but still full of soupy brown water. "I give up," he says, falls sideways, and rolls on his back.

I pick up the palmetto shovel and am about to take over digging when, for some reason, I think of vinegar and oil salad dressing, and how the vinegar always settles to the bottom. I pick up the empty Gatorade container and begin to bail the muddy water.

More water seeps in, but not faster than I can scoop it out. When there is just a layer of thick mud on the bottom, I sit back and wait.

The python is again trying to work its tail under the gator by lifting and sliding beneath it, but the gator lashes its own tail and knocks the back part of the snake away. Neither moves for a few minutes, then the snake tries again. This time the gator makes the mistake of lifting up and trying to back away. The snake's tail shoots under and curls, making a full 360-degree loop around the gator's middle. In an equally sudden move that makes me jump, the python lifts and rolls the gator up in its coils. I can feel the tightness in my own chest as the snake constricts around the gator's abdomen. I take a couple of quick breaths and imagine I can hear the gator's ribs breaking as its chest caves in.

Andy snores softly. Teapot is asleep in the crook of his neck beneath his left ear.

The hole is full of clear water. I rinse the Gatorade bottle, fill it and hold it up to the light. A few particles float in it, but it is otherwise pretty clear. I let those bits settle to the bottom before starting to drink. When I've finished the first bottle, I refill it, then poke Andy, who opens his eyes and blinks. I hold up the bottle.

"No way." He sits up, then glances at the snake and the gator. The python has let go of the gator's jaw and is wrapped so tightly around its body that only the gator's head and front two legs stick out through the coils. The snake's nose is pressed against the alligator's.

"It looks like it's kissing it," I say.

"It's making sure that it's dead." Andy's face is smeared with mud.

"I wonder if that's where the 'kiss of death' expression comes from?"

Andy is looking at me in a way that makes me blush. "You're really pretty, you know?"

I laugh. "Yeah, right." My hair is matted and snarled, caked with dried scum, and has leaves, twigs, and bits of saw grass caught in the tangles. I have a mirror, but I've purposely avoided looking at it. I don't want to see what I look like.

"What's funny?" Andy asks.

"Nothing. I just kind of wish my parents could see me right now—sitting here with a python getting ready to eat an alligator and looking like the thing from the Black Lagoon myself."

"They'd be proud of you."

I laugh. "If they survived twin heart attacks, they would be. Will your parents be proud of you?"

"After they kill me, maybe." He lies back on the grass. "You shouldn't wear all that makeup like you had on Friday. You're prettier without it."

"Where I go to school, everyone wears makeup."

"Even the boys?"

I smile. "Not all of them."

"So you wear it to fit in?"

That's exactly why I wear it. "No." I feel defensive. "It's just . . ."

"Under all those bug bites, you have nice skin. Makeup should be for old women trying to look young, not young girls trying to look older."

I refill and finish another bottle of water, then refill and hand it to him. "What do you know about it?" Him telling me what I shouldn't or should do irks me. At the same time I know he's right. Why do I slather on all that stuff, anyway? Nothing has changed. I still haven't made a single friend. I pull at my yellow Lance Armstrong bracelet—another attempt to fit in.

"What is that rubber thing, anyway?"

"Nothing. I like wearing makeup, and if I do or don't, it's none of your business. When we're out of here, I'll probably never see you again."

"I'd like to see you again," Andy says. He reaches for my hand.

I jerk away. "Well if you call first, I'll wash my face."

Andy looks hurt, so when he stands and puts his hand out to help me up, I take it.

We stand side by side for a moment, watching the reptiles. Our arms are touching. "I didn't mean that, you know. I'd like to see you again, too." I look at him, then lift up on my tiptoes and tilt my head back. He takes my chin in his big hand, leans, and kisses me. It's a long, warm, soft kiss, and my first. "We'd better get going," he whispers. His eyes are still closed, his hand cups my cheek.

I nod as heat spreads from my toes to the top of my head.

Andy drops his hand. "We're losing daylight." He drains the water bottle, refills it, then we share it until it's empty again.

"I want a picture of you and the python and the alligator." I get the camera out, step back and focus, but I'm not sure how to make Andy sharp when he's close to me, and the reptiles sharp when they are farther away. I choose the reptiles, and hope Andy's not blurry.

"Let me take one of you."

He reaches for the camera, but I twist away. "No way. You could blackmail me for life with a picture of me looking like this."

"You'll wish you had one one day when you're telling your grandkids about this."

"I'll live with the regret." I bounce up and down so he can hear my stomach slosh.

Andy fills the bottle one more time, and I put Teapot and the camera in the backpack.

We stand for a moment and watch the python uncoil itself from around the crushed body of the gator.

"Being caught and killed isn't at all like it looks on TV."

Andy shrugs. "I wouldn't know."

"It takes so long."

The python opens its mouth and starts to fit its head over the dead alligator's snout.

"How is it going to eat something that is ten times bigger than its head?"

"Snakes can unhook their jaws. It will pull itself over the gator like putting on a sock."

"It could have been one of us, you know."

"Yeah, but it wasn't." He slides his arms through the backpack straps. "Let's get moving."

After we plow through the muddy perimeter of the hammock, I stop to catch my breath and look back a last time. The gator's whole head is inside the python's. I can see the outline of the bulbous tip of its snout poking up through the snake's skin like knuckles in a glove.

14

Once we're off the trail and out onto the prairie, we turn south and parallel the trees for a while. It takes us about an hour to round the tip of the island. I'm following right behind Andy, but watching my feet, so I only look up when he stops. In front of us the saw grass is taller and denser than any we've seen. It forms a barrier to the east.

"I don't know why it grows like this," Andy says. It's almost an apology.

We stand looking at the golden wall. "I do."

"You do, huh?" He kind of smiles.

"We stopped at a pumping station yest... *Not yesterday*... day before yesterday. It's caused by the sugar growers. The fertilizer they use gets into the water and fertilizes everything. It's like the saw grass and cattails are on steroids. We could just keep going south for a while."

"Look at it. I can't see an end, and it looks like it curves back to the west. We have to go through it."

"But how? We'll be cut to pieces."

Andy slips the backpack off, hands it to me, then steps to the edge of the stand, turns, crosses his arms over his chest and falls backwards into the grass. He stands and does it again, then again, until he's flattened the beginning of a path through it. I follow, walking high and dry, holding my arms out for balance.

For another hour we walk blind, no horizon visible, boxed in by the razor-edged grass. Wading has been slow going, but following Andy's path through the saw grass is harder. I keep losing my balance, falling, and cutting my hands and knees. It feels like I have a million paper cuts.

Every once in awhile the saw grass ends, replaced by cattails that surround a gator hole. We have to cross it, wade through the cattails, and be faced with more tall, dense saw grass. Andy keeps looking at the sun and adjusting our direction.

I'm so tired from the effort I can't keep my footing for more than a few feet. When I fell the first time, I twisted to keep from landing on Teapot, who was riding in the sling around my neck. After that, I put her in the top of the pack. At least when I fall it's forward, so I don't have to worry about squishing her.

It must be about three o'clock when we begin to hear thunder again. Before long, even surrounded by saw grass, we can see the towering top of the approaching storm.

Once it blots out the sun, we can't be sure which direction we're walking.

I focus on keeping my balance, but look up now and then to track the storm. This time when I glance up, I see Andy put something in his mouth. First the Gatorade; now he's got food he's hiding from me.

"What are you eating?"

"Nothing."

"You're chewing something."

"I'm chewing chunks of my belt."

"Why?"

"I'm trying to trick my stomach."

"How's it working?"

"Not great. Want some?"

"Yeah."

At the next gator hole, we rest at the edge of it and, after making plenty of racket to ensure the owner isn't sleeping on the muddy bottom, let Teapot out to feed. I clean the poop out of the backpack, wash the blood off my hands, and spit out the chunk of belt. I felt so full after drinking all that water, but that was hours ago, and I've peed it all away. Now having the flat, leathery taste in my mouth only makes me think more about food, not less. I can't think of anything else, though not the food I really love to eat, like Chinese and Thai. All I can think about is the breakfast I pushed away at the Miccosukee Indian restaurant. What I'd give now for burned eggs, undercooked shredded potatoes, greasy, half-raw bacon, and fried pumpkin bread.

The sky is growing darker. In the distance, toward Naples, lightning flashes in jagged lines, sometimes to the ground and sometimes between thunderheads like they are at war with each other.

My mother is afraid of thunderstorms and has rules: Don't take a bath or talk on the phone or stand near a window or under a tree and certainly don't be in water—the absolute best conductor of electricity. Now here we are, with thunderheads black as tar on the bottom, towering white and puffy on the tops, so high that airplanes headed for Miami International have to fly around them. Though there's no place to hide, I still have to ask, "What are we going to do about that?" I hitch a thumb toward the monstrous cloud.

"Not much we can do."

"We shouldn't be in the water."

"I know, but where are we not in the water?"

"We could lie in the saw grass."

"That's not really out of the water. I don't think a few inches of grass will make any difference, but we can if you want to."

If I was home, I'd be happy it was going to rain. I love to watch the hot summer sky turn black with the promise of a cooling rain. It's so curious to me that as soon as the rain starts, the sky goes from black to gray, as if the clear raindrops contain the color. I try to imagine black raindrops.

Here, where every lightning strike is visible, I feel as wimpy as my mother—and we all tease her when she screams every time it thunders. The storm, coming from the northwest, is nearly on top of us, but the sun is still shining in the southwest sky. The saw grass looks like spun gold beneath the black clouds.

The lightning and claps of thunder are constant. After one particularly loud boom, a flock of white ibis— maybe thirty birds—takes off and flickers in the sunlight, swirling with indecision. Their white bodies against the pitch-dark sky look like someone drawing circles in a dark room with a burning sparkler. "Andy, look."

"What?"

"Aren't they beautiful?"

"That flock of Chokoloskee chickens?" he says.

"I mean the way the sunlight is hitting them."

"Yeah. I guess. The young ones are good eating."

We stand and watch the birds wheeling and turning as the rain, like a gray curtain, comes at us across the prairie. I'm filled with the hopeless urge to try to outrun it. Impossible even if my feet didn't hurt so bad I can barely stand. Thunder booms again, and the sky goes white with another flash of lightning. If I'm going to die, at least I won't be able to feel my feet anymore, and those beautiful birds will be my last memory.

As quickly as we can, we move toward the next thick wall of saw grass. Andy gets there first and launches himself into the stand. I crawl in beside him just as the sky opens and the deluge begins. We turn on our sides, face to face, with Teapot in the pack between us. Andy puts his arm across my shoulder. "You're bleeding," he says.

I shiver and nod.

We both cringe when the next lightning bolt strikes. It seems to just miss us. Thunder crashes so loudly, I throw my arms over my head. The raindrops are large, heavy, surprisingly cold, and they hurt. To lie exposed, as we are, is like being hit with pebbles. The blood on my arms and legs begins to dilute until my skin has a reddish wash.

With the rain come gusty winds. I shiver uncontrollably. Andy rubs my arm. "I'm really sorry about getting you into this, you know?"

"I know." My teeth are chattering. "My father says what doesn't kill us makes us stronger. I'm gonna look forward to that, aren't you?"

Just as I say that, lightning blazes over our heads like a meteor passing. I grab Andy's arm and squeeze my eyes shut. When I open them a moment later, Andy grins at me. I smack him. "Some things deserve being scared of."

"I know."

We both doze off while the storm blows itself out. It's the sun coming out again and its heat on my arm that wakes me.

Andy saws off two chunks of his belt, one of which I take just to keep my mouth from feeling so dry. We plunge out of the saw grass and start east again.

It's probably four-thirty when Andy holds his hand up. I close the gap between us.

"What?"

He's shading his eyes and squinting at the sun.

"Look over there." He points west.

I'm resting, bent over with my hands on my knees. I glance where he's pointing. "I don't see anything."

"There's a plane on the horizon. They've started looking for us."

15

"That dot's a plane?" Only the sunlight off its wings when it banks catches my eye. "How do you know it's looking for us?"

"Because it's flying back and forth. I was watching it before the storm hit."

I'm thrilled. "Why didn't you tell me?"

"What for? No sense getting excited."

"How long do you think it will take them to get here?"

He snorts. "Next week."

"Be serious."

"I am serious."

"Well, let's head that way."

"No. We have to stay on this course. They aren't going to find us today. It will be dark in a few hours.

Unless someone finds the flight bag, they aren't going to get this far north tomorrow either. We'll be on the levee and headed home long before they spot us."

The ray of hope that the sight of the plane brought drains away, taking what little strength I have left with it. "I need to rest, Andy."

"I know. Me, too. Let's head for that cypress stand. There might even be a bit of dry land there to dig another scratch well."

While we were watching the plane, I'd let Teapot out for a swim and a snack. I guess I turn my head too quickly when I glance around to see where she's gone, because I'm suddenly dizzy. I put my hand out for balance but tip sideways and fall over.

"What happened?" He comes back to help me up.

"I feel really light-headed."

"Blood sugar," he says.

"Thanks, doc."

"Want me to carry the duck?"

"She'd probably be safer." I hand the pack to Andy.

We reach the cypress head just before dark. There are no large trees and no dry, open ground, at least not on this side—just plenty of mosquitoes.

I know I used too much of the bug spray last night and after the storm, but when I take the can out of the pack, it feels empty. I shake it, then take the lid off.

"Wait," Andy says. "Save that for tonight."

"This is tonight."

"No. For later, after we've found someplace to sleep. Give me your bandana." We're waist-deep in a swampy pond surrounded by a dense circle of skinny cypress trees.

"Where are we going to sleep? Is there another rookery nearby?"

"Not that I know of, and I haven't seen any birds fly by except ones headed in the other direction." Andy rinses the bird poop out of my bandana.

"What are we going to do now?"

"Rest for a while. If we get on our knees the water will cover us to our chins, and if we put our heads together, I think the bandana will cover both of our faces."

"What about Teapot?"

"She can get under there with us."

"Where's the owner of this hole?"

"This isn't a gator hole. Too shallow. It's a natural pond."

"Are you sure?"

"Yes, and even if it was a gator hole, it could have been dug years ago. There's no reason for gators to be in them this time of year."

"We chased a gator out of nearly every other hole we've seen. Why is this one the exception?"

He ignores me and sinks into the black water. "You coming?"

Mosquitoes are biting my ears, lips, and eyelids, which is worse than the thought of being eaten by a gator, though I can't say I feel the same about being squeezed to death by a python. I sink to my chin in the water, which means sitting on the mushy bottom. I call Teapot, and Andy covers our heads with the bandana.

We stay like that a long time, cheek to cheek with Teapot, her head lodged between her wings, floating at the tips of our noses. Every breath fills my lungs with her wet-pillow smell.

Maybe an hour passes—it's hard to tell—when Andy suddenly jerks the bandana off.

"What?"

"Look." He points through the trees at a small sliver of light.

We both stare for a minute. It seems to be moving closer, but I can't tell if the leaves flickering in the breeze just make it look like it's coming toward us.

"Do you think it's a search party?"

"No. I think it might be someone out frogging, or . . ."

"Hello," I call.

"Shhhh," Andy whispers.

"Why?"

"It might be a poacher."

"What would he be poaching?"

"Gators. Bears. Panthers. Orchids. Who knows."

"Orchids?"

"Keep your voice down. They get big bucks for ghost orchids. Or they could be hunters."

"I thought the season hadn't started."

"It hasn't. That's the point."

"Let's just sit tight until they're close enough for us to see what they're doing." We cover our heads again. Through the material of the bandana I can see the light getting brighter, coming closer.

"If it's a poacher, would he kill us?"

"Who knows? They ain't Boy Scouts."

Whoever they are, they're approaching in total silence, no sound at all. By now I think we should be able to hear the pole hitting the side of their boat or at least the drip of water as the pole is pushed into the muddy bottom, brought out, and pushed in again. Instead, nothing disturbs the never-ending whine of mosquitoes.

"We could tell them our parents will pay a reward," I whisper against Andy's ear. "We could call to him, and if it turns out he's poaching, we'll tell him about the reward."

"It's easier to see gators at night, not quite as simple to catch them. Poachers usually work in pairs, so it's not likely that it's just one person in that boat."

There are the usual night calls: frogs croaking, the barred owls, crickets, Teapot's sleepy little peeps; none are much comfort as we wait for either rescuers or poachers.

"What if they're headed right here?" I whisper.

"Shhh. Even whispers carry over water."

"Then why can't we hear them?"

The bandana moves when Andy shakes his head.

A few more minutes pass. "Damn," Andy says out loud.

My heart skips. "Poachers?"

Andy takes the bandana off. "See for yourself."

The trees are dense, young, and spindly. It takes me a moment to realize that the sliver of light we've been watching is the moon rising. Tears come. I can't help it. I had let myself hope that even if they were poachers, they'd want to help us.

"Are you crying?" Andy asks.

"No."

"Your face is wet."

"I can't take another step, and I know we have to."

"I feel the same way, but we can't stay here."

"You think I don't know that?" *If I ever get out of this . . .* The memory of Mr. Vickers standing at the screen door of the cabin, his face full of concern, comes to me. The guilt and regret I suddenly feel are crushing. It had been a tiny little lie, just because I wanted a couple of hours of fun and maybe to make a friend. Now look at us. *Up to our asses in alligators. Isn't that the expression?* If I had an ounce of humor left, I might have smiled.

Andy scoops a sleepy Teapot up and packs her away.

It's a beautiful night, with enough breeze to keep the mosquitoes thinned out once we're away from the trees. The night is the most beautiful I can remember, and I realize, as I traipse along in Andy's wake, that I've let go of some of my fears. Every step the first day was terrifying. Now, even with the moon, there are stars. More stars than I've ever seen in Miami, where sometimes Orion, the Big Dipper, and Venus seem alone in the sky. In an odd way, I'm beginning to feel a part of this place. The birds, frogs, turtles, snakes, bright green chameleons, even small gators fleeing at our approach makes me sad—like I'm a monster.

By moonlight, we work our way up the east side of the cypress head, looking for a tree with a sturdy trunk and low branches. We've almost reached the tip when Andy lets out a whoop.

All I see is a dead tree with a few bare branches—a stick figure with bony arms held up in distress, as if someone has a gun stuck in its ribs. At the very top is a coffeepot like the ones in old westerns. The bottom's rusted away, and someone has jammed it over the tip of the main trunk. The tree is tall. With the coffeepot on top, it looks like a long-faced cowboy: the spout is a small nose, and the lid up looks as if his hat is pushed back on his head. I think it's creepy looking in the moonlight, but Andy's excited to see it.

"What's with the pot?"

He turns and grins. "That pot's been there since before I was born. It marks where the main east-west, north-south airboat trails cross."

"Will airboats be by here in the morning?"

"No. It only means I know where we are."

"Why won't airboats come by?" "For one thing, tomorrow is Monday. All the weekenders have gone home. Hunting season don't start for two weeks, we're too far north for the tour operators, and in water too shallow for fishermen."

"All right. All right. You can't blame me for asking."

"What it does mean is that we're only about two or three miles from the levee."

"How far did we come today?"

"Five. Six, maybe."

"Wow." Even I have to smile. "We could be on the levee by noon tomorrow. Right?"

"Maybe."

"So why wouldn't we be out tomorrow instead of Tuesday?"

"We'll get there tomorrow, but there's no telling what time, or how far we have to walk once we are on it. If it gets dark before we reach the trail, we can't sleep on the levee. Either way, if they don't find us before dark, we'll have to get back in the water."

"Why can't we sleep on the levee?"

"Pygmy rattlesnakes."

"Don't tell me there are so many rattlesnakes that it's not safe to sleep on the levee."

"Okay."

"Okay, what?"

He looks at me. "I won't tell you."

"So there are?"

"Like worms."

"God, Andy."

He turns and smiles at me. "Worry about tomorrow tomorrow."

. . .

About thirty minutes later, we come to a small hammock with a big, strong pond-apple tree growing at the edge. Andy uses the butcher knife like a machete to cut away the smaller branches along its multiple trunks, swinging the blade like a samurai warrior and grunting like de-twigging the tree is the heat of battle. There are palmettos growing nearby, and he cuts a bunch of the big, fan-shaped leaves, layering them into the crotch where three limbs split off and making what resembles a chair.

"That's nice. Where are you going to sleep?" I'm kind of kidding, but there really isn't room in the tree for the two of us.

"Lying down," he says, making his hands into a stirrup.

I put a dripping boot in his hands, grab a branch, and let him boost me into the palmetto nest.

"How's that?"

"Like my dad's old recliner." It isn't, of course. My butt's pinched between two limbs, and the one behind my back will be like sleeping against a lamppost. "What do you mean lying down?"

He hands me Teapot in the backpack. "There." He points to the thick mud at the edge of the hammock.

"You're kidding?"

"I am not." He wades across mud, which makes sucking sounds and smells rotten. Once he's ashore, he starts whacking away at the palmetto again. When he has about a dozen more leaves, he spreads them out across the mud and lies down.

"What if a python comes?"

He holds the knife up and turns it so the moon reflects off the blade.

I hang my boots on the tips of two branches, pull my socks off and drape them nearby. Both my feet show white in the moonlight, with fissures and cracks. They sting in the cool night air, and when I accidentally get bug spray in the broken blisters, my eyes tear with pain.

DAY FOUR

16

Teapot's alarmed peeping wakes me just before dawn. I'm frozen in place and so confused it takes a second for me to realize a snake is moving up the branch the backpack hangs on.

"Andy!" I scream; then at the snake, "Get away!" I flip my hand at it. The snake's tongue tastes the air as it moves up through the straps and around the pack.

"Andy." I twist to look over my shoulder. He's gone, but he must have slept there; mud has oozed through the seams of the palmetto leaves. I surprise myself by not assuming he's been eaten. Of course, there are no signs of struggle.

The snake is almost to the gap between the zippers when I hear Andy in the water. He's yards away.

"There's a snake after Teapot."

"You have to grab it."

"I can't."

"You have to."

The snake's tongue is flicking in and out of the gap.

Andy tries to run, but I know he can't get here in time. The snake's head disappears into the pack. Teapot's peeps reach a high pitch.

"Catch it behind its head. When he feels you touch him, get ready, because he'll yank his head out of the pack and wrap his body around your arm. Don't freak. He won't be able to bite you."

I gulp my fear and grab the snake. Its does exactly what Andy said it would. Its powerful muscles ripple and twitch as it tries to pull its head out of my fist. I'm aware of how dry and cool its skin feels, not at all slimy like I'd expected. "Now what?"

Andy's almost beside me. "Just hang on to it."

"Don't worry." I have no intention of letting go.

I wonder if, when it was climbing the tree, it crossed me, tasting my skin as it worked its way up through the branches. What amazes me is that I don't feel the same revulsion I felt two days before at the cabin. I knew it wasn't a poisonous snake the minute I saw it. It's almost identical to the one in the outhouse—a corn snake, I think Andy said. This one is reddish with black triangular markings. The one in the outhouse had been more orange.

Andy reaches up and puts his hand over mine, catching the snake behind its head. When he unwraps it from my arm, its tail whips and hooks a branch. "Take the pack and get down. When you're out of the way, I'll let it go."

I study Andy's grip on the snake. "Are you proud of me?"

"Very."

"It felt cool to touch." I reach and run a finger up its body.

"Don't go against the scales. Stroke with them. You can hurt him otherwise." He holds it up so its silvery underside is facing me. "Feel his belly. It's like silk."

The snake has relaxed. I hope it's because it knows we aren't going to hurt it. I run the tips of my fingers along its stomach and feel it quiver. "I'd like to hold it again, if you don't think it will bite me."

"He'll only bite if he feels threatened. They're very gentle. But you have to support his body and his head, and promise you won't freak and drop him."

"I promise."

"And he's strong, so you have to hold him just tight enough but not too tight, okay? If you hold him too tight, it will frighten him and he'll start thrashing around."

"Andy, I get it. Even if he whips around and bites me, I won't drop him or squeeze too tightly. I want to do this. I'm sick of being afraid." I reach and tease his tail loose from the branch with a finger, then put my hand and arm under it to support his five-foot-long body. When I nod, Andy lets go of his head. I'd made a noose with my thumb and forefinger, but it isn't snug enough to hold his head.

The back half of the snake is wrapped around my arm, but the front half pulls loose and whips back and forth like a dropped air hose.

Andy steps up on a lower limb to try and catch his head, but I turn so he misses.

"It's okay," I say. I can feel the snake's muscles tense and ease. His tongue flicks in and out, but when he turns to taste my face, my heart begins to rocket around in my chest, and when his tongue brushes my cheek, a chill runs through me. I turn my head to let his tongue tickle my nose. I have to cross my eyes to focus as the snake slides across my shoulder, passing under my hair and onto the branch behind my head. He keeps going until only the tip of his tail is crooked around my wrist. I hold still for a moment; then, with a final flick of his tail, he lets go of me. I look at Andy and grin. "That was awesome."

Andy smiles. "I told you." He unzips the pack and lets Teapot out. "We'd better get going."

"Did you see him lick me? Was that to see if I was edible?"

"He knew you weren't edible."

I balance myself on a branch and try to pat the flaps of skin that are peeling off yesterday's shiny new blisters back into place before putting the socks and boots on. When I'm ready, I put my hands on his shoulders and let him lift me out of the tree. As he lowers me into the water, I kiss his cheek.

"What was that for?"

"I don't know exactly. Maybe just for putting up with me."

An odd, sad look crosses his face.

"What?"

"Nothing. It's nice of you to say, that's all." Andy squeezes my hand, then turns and begins to move toward shore.

"Where are you going?"

"I found some dry ground and was going to dig another scratch well when I heard you calling."

He's not wearing his T-shirt. I wonder where it is, but am more curious about the snake. "So what was he doing when he licked me?" I follow him, and Teapot follows me.

"He wasn't licking you, he was tasting you. Snakes have a gland in the roof of their mouths. The tongue picks up molecules of scent that are carried back to that gland. Snakes are deaf, and they don't see like we do either. They pick up on movement and on the heat birds and mammals give off. That's how he knew there was a meal in the backpack."

That's almost as many words as Andy has strung together since I met him. "How do you know all this?" I ask to keep him talking.

"I had a pet corn snake once. I read all about them in a library book."

"What did you feed it?" "Baby ducks."

I hit him.

"It lived in the airboat shed, and it ate whatever it wanted: mice, rats, who knows."

"How can you call it a pet if you didn't keep it in anything?"

"It would let me pick it up and stuff. I had a pet purple gallinule too, and they migrate. It would come back every year. If something trusts you enough, you don't have to keep it in a cage."

I look at Teapot, crossing the mud in little starts and stops. I take a step and she runs to catch up, but we're leaving deep footprints in the mud and she keeps falling into them, then has to right herself, climb out and run to catch us. I wait until she bumps against my ankle, pick her up, and cup her to my cheek. My heart aches.

"I know most of the birds I've seen out here, but what's a purple gallinule?"

"They look a little like a coot, but they're purplish-blue with yellow legs, long toes for walking on lily pads, and a beak that looks like candy corn."

The mention of candy makes my mind reel. A third day without food. I look down at my concave stomach and knobby hip bones showing through my wet, muddy shorts.

Andy's T-shirt is on the shore and looped over a branch like he'd hung it to dry. He sees me looking at it. "I was catching fish."

"With what?"

"My shirt."

I must look baffled.

"I bent a willow branch, put my T-shirt over it, and was using it like a net."

"Did you catch anything?" I'm imagining making fire like they do on *Survivor* and cooking his catch.

"Just a few minnows..." He looks sheepish. "I ate them."

"Alive?"

"And still wiggling."

I grimace.

"It wasn't much worse than swallowing a pill. Want me to catch you some?"

"I don't think I can eat a live fish."

There are reeds growing through clear water. I suppose I've been so focused on looking out for snakes and alligators that I haven't noticed there are minnows everywhere. They are tiny, about the length of the tip of my pinky finger. "You ate some of those?" I point at the baby fish.

"Not enough to make a difference."

He sinks the shirt-covered hoop in the water and holds it steady just beneath the surface. After a few minutes, a half dozen minnows swim back, curious, I guess, about whether it's something to eat. They are joined by few little black tadpoles with long tails.

Andy holds his net steady, puts his thumb in his mouth, bites off a piece of cuticle, then spits it into the water covering the net. The minnows and tadpoles attack the little piece of skin, and Andy lifts the hoop so slowly at first that the fish aren't aware that they are caught until the water drains through the fabric, leaving them flipping and flopping in the air. He holds it out to me. "Help yourself."

"You first."

Andy pinches two tiny fish and a tadpole between his thumb and forefinger, tilts his head back, opens his mouth, and drops them in. He swallows quickly, gives his head a shake, then holds the rest out to me. I pick a fish up, bring it to my nose and smell it. I've always done that. Smelled new things before I taste them. It doesn't smell fishy; it smells like the water. I think about what it will feel like to put it in my mouth, feel it wiggle. I also imagine it isn't going to do a thing to make my stomach hurt less. It may even make it worse. I lower my hand until it is under water. The little minnow swims in the bowl of my cupped hand until it can get over the rim and swim into the reeds.

"Chicken," Andy says.

"I let it go for my karma."

He's eaten all the rest, a dozen or more. "Karma! What is that anyway?"

I think he's kidding, so I don't answer. "Feel better?"

"Worse. The more I eat the more I want."

On the inside, I smile. *Karma.*

. . .

Andy takes his shirt off the hoop, puts it on, wades ashore and cuts and trims another palmetto leaf to use as a shovel. We take turns digging the hole, then sit on the bank to take turns bailing muddy water out until it begins to run clear.

"Is your dad on a business trip to Miami?" I ask to kill time and to take my mind off my empty stomach.

A funny look crosses Andy's face. "I guess you could call it that."

"What does he do?"

"Let's just say he's between prospects."

He's being cryptic. "Did he go there to look for a job?"

"I don't think so."

"Too bad. If he found something, maybe you'd move."

"Yeah. Like that's ever going to happen. You couldn't pry him out of the 'Glades with a crowbar."

We each drink as much as we can, then I wade in to collect Teapot while Andy fills the bottle for the rest of the day.

We pass the pond apple again on our way out of the hammock. The snake is making its way down through the branches, gliding like a ribbon. When I turn to follow Andy, it occurs to me that I may never see anything like this again, and for some reason that makes me think of our kiss. A person only gets to have one first of anything.

"Watch your head." Andy ducks as he crosses under the biggest spider web I've ever seen. It's stretched between two spindly cypress trees about nine feet apart. A black-and-yellow spider like the one in the outhouse is in the center. Andy plows on but I stop. A million dewdrops are caught on the strands of silk. Each one reflects the sun's rays in blues, greens, and reds. I find it hard to breathe.

The morning sun also colors the saw grass to a rich golden yellow, and ahead of us for as far as I can see, small, square, dew-covered spider webs are draped like a thousand silver hammocks. It looks as if they drifted down during the night and came to rest on the tips of the short saw-grass clumps. Mist rises off the water. I think of my mom, whose most prized possession is a large book on the French Impressionists that she bought at a yard sale. "Mom would say this looks like a Monet morning."

"That's nice," Andy mutters. He is staring at the western horizon. "They got an early start."

"Who?" I ask before looking up. A small plane is making loops back and forth, closer than yesterday.

"And look there." Andy points.

Farther west is a Coast Guard helicopter.

"They haven't found where we left from, have they?"

"Not even close," Andy says.

"You were right, weren't you?"

"About what?"

"How long it would have taken them to find us— me—if I'd stayed at the cabin."

"Yeah, but about now we could set it on fire, and they would figure it out."

"If we'd had matches."

We walk on for a while. "I know this isn't right to say, but it's kind of nice to have people looking for us, isn't it?"

"Speak for yourself."

I catch his arm. "What does that mean?"

"They're looking for you."

"That doesn't make sense. They have to be looking for *us*, both of us. How would they know I was out here if they hadn't figured out we're together? In fact," I say, "they may just be looking for you and looking for me someplace else."

He puts a finger to his lips. "Listen."

I hear an engine, but far away. "Is that the helicopter?"

"No, damn it, that's an airboat."

"Why damn it?"

"I should have left something at the coffeepot to let them know we'd been there."

"What would we have left? All we have is the backpack and my bandana."

"I don't know. Something."

"Does it make sense to go back and wait there?" "Too far, and it's not where they're looking. We could be waiting all day, maybe two. They're bound to have a grid they're working. We're better off if we stick to the plan."

I salute him. "Aye, aye, captain."

"Funny."

I glance a last time at the planes and feel terrible guilt for my thoughts of a moment before. To take any pleasure in making people worry is bad for *my* karma.

I imagine the terror my parents feel not knowing if I'm dead or alive. I try to remember if I left any clue behind that would suggest I was somewhere in the Everglades rather than the latest victim of an abduction. They're probably thinking I went for a walk and some Loop Road maniac got me.

We slog forward for another hour in silence. The sun gets hot quickly; my thirst returns, and I'm so hungry my head begins to pound.

"Oh my God. Look." Andy, who's about ten yards ahead of me, points at something to our south. I shade my eyes but don't see anything.

He starts to run as fast as the water level will let him, waving his arms over his head and shouting. Birds scream and rise into the air in front of him.

I try to follow, but my feet cripple me. Andy falls, gets up, runs a few more yards, trips and falls again. I still don't see what he's after. He's pretty far away when he stops. He looks around as if he's confused about the direction to take, then hangs his head for a few moments, turns, and starts back toward me.

"What did you see?" I ask when he's close enough to hear me.

"Nothing." He looks as if he might cry.

I touch his arm. "What did you think you saw?"

He glances at where he'd stopped running. "I saw two men sitting on stools or something, and I saw smoke rising from their fire and I smelled fish frying."

He shakes his head. "When I got there, it was a shrub with one bare branch sticking up."

"I'm sorry." I hug him.

"I really could smell fish frying."

"I know. I thought I smelled pumpkin bread yesterday." I pat his back. "How 'bout another sliver of that nutritious, delicious belt of yours?"

By noon the sun is brutal. No clouds. No breeze. We come to another tree island and decide to take a break. I let Teapot out and watch as she swims in speedy, thrilled little loops through lily pads the size of hubcaps and the small reeds at one edge of a pond before starting to eat. I stay nearby with as much of myself underwater as I can get. I used the last of the bug spray last night, figuring that if I could keep the mosquitoes away long enough to fall asleep, I'd be too dead to the world to notice them when it wore off.

We sink into the shallow water at the edge of the island and sit back to back to support each other. Andy starts to snore right away. I'm afraid I'll fall asleep, too, so I call Teapot and get her settled in the backpack before I close my eyes.

I'm not sure what woke me, but I feel someone watching us. My eyes pop open. There's no one there, but the sun is lower and the usual rain clouds are building in the west. It's two o'clock, is my guess.

Teapot's scratching and peeping in the backpack, which I'd hung off the limb of a nearby tree. In the water just below the shaking, wiggling pack are the eyes I'd sensed watching us. Two eyes and nostrils just above the water line. "Dream on," I say to the little four-foot-long gator.

"What?" Andy mutters and then goes back to snoring.

"There's a little gator here with us," I whisper, trying not to frighten it. I wonder if they're deaf, too, like snakes, then decide that wouldn't make any sense. What use would all the racket males make be if the females couldn't hear them? "Are you awake?" I ask.

The gator turns a little, but Teapot's gyrations have its full attention.

I lean forward, throwing Andy off balance. He wakes with a start and splashes to regain his balance. The gator spins and swims into some reeds.

"You scared our company away."

"What company?" He rubs his eyes.

"A little gator was eyeballing Teapot."

He stood up. "How little?" "Why?"

"Because baby gators usually have a big mother guarding them. Was it black and yellow?"

"No. It was gray and three or four feet long."

"Good." He holds his hand out. "We've burned a lot of daylight, let's get moving." He seems cranky and short-tempered. Hungry beyond words, no doubt. I certainly am.

I have always been a picky eater. Never again, I vow. "I need to let Teapot out to eat a little." I wonder if I could eat algae and duckweed like Teapot and not get sick.

"It takes too long."

"What's the matter with you? Why are you acting mad at me?"

"We're wasting time, that's all."

"Go on ahead then. I'll let her eat and catch up."

"Do you know how slow I'm walking already so you don't fall behind?"

"Well, please don't do me any favors."

"I'm responsible for getting you out of here."

"Well, you are sure as hell responsible for getting me in," I snap.

"If you'd worn what I told you to wear, you'd be able to keep up."

"If you'd told me I'd be boating in and walking out, I would have adhered to the dress code."

Andy turns and heads out.

"Tell Daddy bye-bye," I tell Teapot, waving at his back.

I let him get a few yards out in front, then I follow. When I'm far enough from the little gator, I let Teapot out of the pack.

She's famished and turns butt-up immediately in search of food. She seems to like mushy vegetation. I walk slowly, staying close to her and keeping a sharp eye out for snakes and alligators while watching how far ahead Andy's getting. I catch him glancing over his shoulder to check on me, too. When I wave, he turns away quickly.

Thunder rumbles nearer. This time, unless we make the levee, there will be no saw grass dense enough to climb into.

When I decide that Andy is too far ahead, I call Teapot and bed her down in the pack. When I look up again, Andy has stopped and is waiting for me. "Are you through acting like a snot," I shout.

If he hears me, he doesn't answer, just turns and starts walking. A few minutes later, I hear a choked-off scream.

17

The levee. He's spotted the levee, but the hair on the nape of my neck reacts differently. It was not a cry of joy. He didn't shout; he screamed. And he's standing absolutely still, not waving for me to come on. Something's wrong. I try to run, but there's nothing left in my legs.

Andy's standing at the edge of a clump of cattails.

"Is it the levee?" I call, cupping a hand to my mouth.

He doesn't answer or even look around, as if he can't hear me.

"Thanks for waiting," I say when I finally catch up. I'm hoping that's why he's standing there.

The cattails he's in are at the edge of a wide canal. The chalk-white levee rises steeply on the opposite side. Tears swim in my eyes. I look at Andy and grin. "We made it."

Sweat beads on his forehead and runs in streaks down the side of his face. Only his hand, which he holds behind his back, moves as he motions for me to slow down. "Don't come any closer," he whispers.

My body tenses, and even in this scorching heat, chill bumps spread down my arms and legs. Something *is* wrong. "Why are you standing there like that?" One foot is in the weeds, the other is a little forward and looks caught up in the dead cattails around his ankle.

The cattail moves. "Oh, my God." It's a snake, and it's circling his right ankle. "Is that a water moccasin?"

"Yes."

"It's not very big."

"The young ones are just as deadly," he whispers.

"You said snakes are deaf, right?"

"Yeah. Why?"

"You're whispering."

"I guess I am."

"How'd it get there?"

"I was waiting for you to catch up, put my foot here to clean the cattails off—and there it was."

The moccasin, firmly coiled around Andy's ankle, stops moving.

"What's it doing?"

"Settling in for a nap, I think."

"Its eyes don't look closed." I can't really tell from this distance.

"They don't have eyelids."

"How long do snakes sleep?"

"If it just ate it could be hours."

"You're kidding."

"No."

Andy looks tippy. His right leg is directly in front of his left.

I move closer, watching carefully where I step in case there's a nest of them nearby. "How long can you stand off-balance like that?"

"I hope longer than he can nap."

Here and there are chunks of limestone from the blasting out of the canal. I take off the backpack, climb up, and sit down on one of them. "How can you be so calm?"

"What choice do I have?"

"I don't know, but I don't think I could just stand there."

"Then I guess it's a good thing he chose me instead of you."

"Are you still mad at me?"

"No."

"You sound mad."

"I have a poisonous snake wrapped around my ankle, for Christ's sake. How would you sound?"

"Scared."

"Okay, then."

I remember when we saw the moccasin at Shark Valley, Mr. Vickers said how deadly the bite is depends on how much venom is injected and how far it is to the nearest hospital. I look off to the west where there are now three search planes and a helicopter—all still miles away.

"You'd think one of them would come over here. Why wouldn't they think the way you did and guess that we'd head for the levee?"

"I don't know. I'm sure they've got a plan and are sticking to it just like we did."

"You want to talk or something? It might make the time go faster."

"I guess. What do you want to talk about?"

"I don't know." I unzip the pack, wide enough to stick my hand inside. I want to touch Teapot, to feel her soft, warm body against my hand. "So you said you don't have any brothers or sisters, right?"

"My parents couldn't have children."

"You mean any more children?"

"No, any. I'm adopted. My mother is really my aunt. Her sister is my birth mother."

"That's kind of weird," I say before I can stop the words.

"Maybe people who live in Coconut Grove don't have illegitimate children? Or is it that they can afford to have abortions?"

"I didn't mean it that way, Andy. I meant that must be strange if you see your mother. Does she live nearby?"

"Nobody knows where she is. As soon as she was able to walk after giving birth to me, she did. No one ever heard from her again. She was a druggie, so maybe she's dead."

"You sound like you don't care whether she is or she isn't."

"Why would I care? She didn't do nothing for me. Like my mother says, she didn't even push. I was a preemie and delivered by C-section."

"At least your aunt . . . your mother loves you."

"My mother loves babies. She's always off helping some woman who needs another kid like she needs a hole in her head to have one more. But I don't think she likes kids past the age of three." He rotates his head like his neck is stiff.

"What makes you say that?"

"I don't know exactly. It seems like once I knew the difference between a coral snake and king snake, I was on my own."

"How do you tell the difference?"

"The coral snake has a black nose and the king snake has a red one, but there's a rhyme she taught me: Red next to black is a friend of Jack. Red next to yellow will kill a fellow."

While we've been talking, the moccasin has shifted slightly, fitting itself more tightly between the top of Andy's sneaker and his anklebone.

"So what *does* your dad do?" I'm still curious about the man who has a Confederate flag hanging in his garage.

"Nothing now," Andy says.

I look up from the snake to his face. "What does that mean? You said he was in Miami on business, right?"

"I said he was in Miami, you jumped to the conclusion it was for business. He's on his monthly trip to check with his P.O."

"Don't you have mail delivery out here?"

Andy glances at me, snorts a laugh, then looks quickly at the snake. "Not since the pony express ran out of horses with webbed hooves. His P.O. is his parole officer. He's an ex-con."

Even though my family lives at the edge of the high-crime section of Coconut Grove, I've never known anyone who's actually been to jail. "What did he do . . . if you don't mind me asking?"

"What else? Drugs."

"Took them or ran them?"

"Ran 'em. He was a stone crab fisherman and knew the mangrove swamps like the back of his hand. He still laughs about how long it took the Feds to catch him. I was six when he got arrested. He's only been out for eight months."

"Can't he go back to fishing?"

"The Feds took his boat. There's no money to buy another one. What does your old man do?"

"He's . . . in construction."

"Rich, in other words?"

I said that wrong. That's how I answer kids at school whose parents are attorneys, professors, and doctors.

"He's a roofer. And my mother works in the cafeteria at school."

"Is your mother's job how you got into such a fancy school?"

"Ha. They're way too posh to take the kid of one of their mashed-potato-scoopers. I'm on a swimming scholarship."

Andy's left leg muscle quivers from the strain of standing like a tightrope walker. "I'm going to have to move," he says. "Hang on." He slowly lifts his arms for balance, then leans forward, shifting his weight to his right leg. I watch the snake to see if it senses Andy's calf muscle flex. His thigh muscle trembles as he twists his left foot in jerky little moves out from directly behind his right.

The snake's head lifts and its tongue slides out.

"Don't move," I whisper, and hold my breath.

Andy closes his eyes when the snake turns and flicks its tongue through the hole in his jeans to the raw, red skin beneath.

I squeeze my eyes shut, too. *Please, God.*

The only sound is the breeze moving the grass and thunder. I open my eyes. The snake's head is back on its top coil.

A great blue heron flies past and down the canal. A fish jumps ahead of its big shadow. My heart slows. "So . . ." I take a deep breath. "Where do you want to go to college?"

"I always thought I'd like to go to Florida State—as far from here as I can get, but I guess that's not going to happen."

"Why not?"

"If we don't have enough money for a boat, how do you think my parents can afford to send me to college?"

"I don't know. You're big and strong. Can't you get a football scholarship or something?"

"How easy was it for you to get a scholarship?"

"Not very."

"Besides, I'm not all that great at sports, and until I'm old enough to drive there's no way to get to practice or the games."

"Well, you shouldn't just give up on the idea of ... Andy, it moved."

"I know. I felt it."

"Looks like it just got more comfortable."

"I'm hoping it will loosen enough for me to kick it off."

The boulder I'm sitting on is cutting into the backs of my legs—like another part of my body hurting matters. I want to shift but am afraid to.

"My parents didn't get to go to college and don't want me or my brother to end up having to work as hard as they do—a notch up from slavery, my dad says. If you don't go to college, what are you going to do?"

"I'll work for my uncle—fishing—until I can save enough to buy my own boat."

Teapot's trying to climb out of the pack. I move my hand so she can stick her head out.

"Have you ever smoked weed?" I ask.

"I've tried it a couple times." Andy says. "Have you?"

"I thought about it once, but I didn't do it."

"Bet those rich kids at your school can buy all the dope they want."

I try to figure out what his tone means. It's not jealousy. Anger, maybe. "Do you blame the people who buy drugs for your dad getting arrested?"

"I don't know. Wouldn't you?"

"Maybe, but didn't he make it easier for them to get it. Besides we're all responsible for the choices we make, aren't we? I'd like to think it's not my fault I'm here. If the other girls had been nice to me, or you hadn't been so charming . . ." I smile, even though his back is to me. "But really, it is my own fault. There's no one else to blame."

The snake hasn't moved a muscle. I can see its sides rising and sinking with each breath.

"What made you decide not to smoke it when you had the chance?" Andy asks.

"I don't have any friends at school."

"I don't believe that."

"It's true though. They look down their noses at me 'cause Mom works in the cafeteria."

"What does any of that have to do with smoking pot?"

"At school, I like to walk down to the bay to study. My favorite spot to sit is in among the giant roots of a banyan tree. I was there one day when a couple of girls from my class walked by. They were headed for the end of the boat dock and didn't see me. They had a joint lit before one of them turned to glance back at the school and saw me.

"You cool?" I imitate her fashionista-girl voice for Andy.

"I'm cool," I'd said, but really I was blown away they'd risk being expelled like that.

"One of them asked me if I wanted a hit. I told her no, thanks, but I actually thought about it for a minute. I want to make friends, but I decided I didn't need one badly enough to risk getting thrown out of the school my parents are so proud I got into."

Thunder rumbles again. I turn to see how close the storm is. Earlier in the day one had rained itself out before reaching us. But now an isolated curtain of rain, with blue sky on either side, is moving toward us. I can smell it coming.

I turn back and glance at Andy's ankle. The snake's head is up, and its ebony tongue is sliding in and out. I touch my cheek where the corn snake's red tongue had brushed my face.

The muscles in Andy's jaw work. His left calf muscle quivers. "I think it smells Teapot," he whispers.

I look down. Teapot is working the zipper-pull back and forth through her bill. I start to push her back into the pack. Why hadn't I thought to use Teapot to lure the snake away before now? "How fast can that snake move?"

"Very fast, but it will move slowly on the hunt. It's the strike that's like lightning, but it can only strike its body length . . . I think."

"How long is that?" Seemed a logical question.

"Not very. Two feet, maybe."

I'm about six feet from Andy. "If I put the pack a little closer, do you think it will let go of you and come after Teapot?"

"It's worth a try."

"I guess we'll find out." I push Teapot's head back inside the pack and close the zipper, then lean over as far as I can and put the pack an arm's length closer to Andy— three feet from the snake.

"When it loosens enough," he says, "I'll kick it off. If it lets go before I can do that, grab the pack and get away."

The moccasin is so obviously toxic that I can't imagine not recognizing the difference between it and the benign brown water snake before now. Its pupils are thin slits like a cat's eye in sunlight. It doesn't have the corn snake's small delicate head. This snake's head is shaped like an arrowhead, with a scaly plate like a hood over the eyes. There are large swellings where I guess the poison is stored, and pits behind its nostrils.

The snake's coils have loosened, and its head is up, tongue sliding in and out.

"Can you see it?"

"Not too good," he says.

"Don't move. It has the tip of its tail coiled around your shoelace."

"Tell me when."

I hold my breath.

Andy tightens his right calf muscle in preparation.

I blink and take a deep breath.

Teapot scratches to get out, peeping.

The snake—for a split second—undoes its tail and lies still across the toe of Andy's tennis shoe.

"Now!"

Andy kicks so hard that the snake sails out over the canal, twisting in midair, trying to strike, its white mouth open, fangs extended. It splashes into the water nearly to the far bank of the canal.

Andy just stands there, looking at where the snake hit the water.

I leap up, fists punching the air. "You rock." I grab and hug him, but when I start to let go, he clings to me; his head is bowed and pressing hard against mine—so hard it hurts. It isn't a hug of joy, quick and full of relief. It's clingy, holding on out of some other emotion. "We shouldn't cross right here, should we?" I say softly. "There's one mad moccasin over there somewhere." I pat his back. Still he holds on. "Andy, are you okay?"

He nods against my shoulder, then lets me go, but doesn't move.

"You owe Teapot an apology for all the bad things you said about her, you know?"

He doesn't smile.

"It's okay to have been scared. I would have been too terrified to hold still."

"I thought the levee was on this side of the canal," he says.

"Oh," I'm confused. "Does it make a difference?"

He shrugs but continues to look at the other side with an odd expression on his face.

18

I watch the water for a minute. When Andy squares his shoulders and starts for the edge, I say, "The current's running north to south."

"So?"

"Why don't we walk north a little ways so that snake is headed one direction and we're headed in the other?"

Andy turns and marches off. I follow, baffled by the way he's acting.

We've gone maybe fifty feet when we come to a nice wide break in the cattails. Andy trudges right past it.

"What's wrong with right here?"

He turns and comes back. "Yeah. This is as good as any."

"What *is* the matter with you? You act like you are disappointed that we've finally made it."

"Nothing." He stands looking at the other side as if it were miles away.

There's a berm on our side of the canal, a ledge no higher than the edge of a swimming pool. I let Teapot out, then sit at the water's edge and take my boots off. I leave Andy's socks on. I don't want to look at the condition my feet are in.

"I'll swim across with Teapot, then you throw our shoes over, okay?"

He doesn't answer.

"Andy?" I touch his arm.

"Yeah." His skin twitches under my touch.

I drop my hand. "That way if you miss, I can swim out and get them."

No answer.

There's a pile of limestone boulders that disappear like a staircase into the dark canal waters. When I step off the berm onto the top of the closest one, even through Andy's socks, it feels like I'm standing in broken glass. I dive into the canal and swim slowly, using the breast-stroke so that Teapot can keep up.

The canal is about the same width as the University of Miami's Aquatic Center pool. I learned to swim there and am not even winded when I reach the other side. I heave myself out onto the embankment, then turn and grin at Andy. "Piece of cake. Now let's see that pitching arm."

Without smiling, he throws the first boot across. It lands in the water at my feet. I only have to lean forward.

"Wow. What a shot," I say as the next one comes sailing across and passes so close to my head that I have to duck. It lands against the steep side of the levee and slides down to stop beside my right hip. "When we get out of here, I'm taking you to a carnival so you can win me a teddy bear."

No reaction.

I can't figure out what's bugging him, but it's beginning to piss me off. He stands staring at the water, maybe to make sure the snake hasn't decided to swim upstream, too. Teapot is safely nestled beside my right ankle, so I flop back against the smashed seashell slope and close my eyes.

A minute or two passes before I hear Andy enter the water. There's splashing, then silence. I roll my head to one side and open my eyes. Only his right hand, holding the pack, sticks out of the water. I sit up. "Andy!"

He's going down. I dive in, swim out to him, and grab the backpack, thinking—stupidly, since there's only the camera, the knife and an empty Gatorade bottle in it—that the weight has pulled him under. I start for the levee with it, but glance back in time to see his hand, in a cascade of air bubbles, slide beneath the surface.

In the water safety course I took years ago, I learned that when someone is drowning, you have to be careful that they don't latch on and drag you down, too. I dive after him. The water is clear, but dark brown. I can only see the white skin of his outstretched palms as he slips toward the bottom. I push the backpack into them. His right hand clamps closed on a strap. Holding the other strap, I kick with all my might against the drag of his weight and pull for the surface with my other arm. It already feels as if my chest will explode, but if I let go, I'll never find him again. There is sunlight above, total darkness below.

The stale air in my lungs puffs out my cheeks and tries to seep through my lips. I swallow it back into my lungs. If I let the air out, I'll have no choice—either drown with Andy or release him. Bright circles of light explode behind my eyes. *I can't make it*, my mind screams as the last of my air ruptures from my nose in a silver bubble. A moment later, my foot strikes one of the limestone boulders piled against the berm side of the canal. I take a step up, grab the backpack strap with both hands and pull as hard as I can, then tip my head back. My face breaks the surface and I gulp air, a great huge lungful.

The backpack goes slack in my hands. He's slipped off.

I leave the pack on the berm, suck in as much air as I can hold, and dive after him. I can see him sliding down like a shadow against the yellowy limestone. My hand and arm look like rust in the tannin-stained water as I reach for him and miss. The pressure makes it feel like my eardrums will burst. I ignore the pain and kick harder.

This time I make a grab for his hair, catch a fistful, turn, and drag him toward the surface. With my hands in his armpits, I back up the side of the boulder, tugging and pulling until his head is out of the water.

I hold him there for a second, gasping for air myself.

The sky opens up and it begins to pour.

"Andy?" His head lolls to the side.

Panic rises like bile. He isn't breathing. "Andy!" I shriek.

I grab his collar, lift, and pull him higher onto the boulder. I feel his shirt tearing as I drag him—like cheese across a grater—up the rock. With an adrenaline-charged burst of strength, I jerk him out of the canal and onto the berm. Grabbing what's left of his belt, I pull him around so that his feet are higher than his head, then roll him over on his stomach, straddle his waist and start pushing on his scraped and bleeding back. Water gushes from his mouth. I push again and again until no more water comes out, then I roll him over, tilt his head back, pinch his nose closed, and put my mouth over his. I blow and see his chest rise. I place two fingers against his throat to feel for the pulse in his neck. To my relief, I find one. I blow more air into his lungs, feel it exit smelling like canal water, then breathe for him again. He suddenly begins to cough and gulp air.

I sit back on my haunches and cover my face with my hands.

He struggles to sit up, choking, his face scarlet. I pound his back, fury rising in me until I'm hitting him as hard as I can. "Why didn't you tell me you couldn't swim?"

He tries to say something, but his voice is raspy and raw. He begins to cough again, so he grabs my wrists and holds them pinched together in his fist. I pull free and throw my arms around him. Teapot waddles up and nestles in beside us.

We sit for a while in the pouring rain with our arms around each other until our breathing is normal again.

"I think you should walk out and bring help back for me," Andy says.

"Andy, I can tow you across the canal. I could have the first time if you'd just told me. What's so frigging macho about drowning?"

"I watched how you did it. It looked easy enough."

"How can you live surrounded by all this water and never learn to swim?"

"It's shallow. Besides, there was never anybody to teach me."

We sit a little longer.

"We need to go, Andy." The rain has stopped.

"I can't, Sarah."

"I'll tow you. It's easy. I learned it in a water safety class. I'll just hook you under the chin and swim us across."

He shakes his head. "You go ahead over and we'll just parallel each other."

"I have to get my feet out of this water." I pull a sock off.

Andy glances at my foot, then quickly looks away.

I'd known it was bad, but it's worse than I imagined. Most of the top layer of skin on my foot is still in the sock. I pull off the other one, then turn them both inside out, lean over the edge of the berm, and dip them in the water. Pieces of skin float off. In few seconds, minnows, hiding in the shallows among the reeds, gather in a feeding frenzy around the strips of flesh. Teapot, curious about the minnows, waddles to the edge, settles into the water, and begins to eat my skin, too.

I wrinkle my nose. "I guess I should be glad it's not going to waste."

. . .

Nothing I say persuades Andy to get back into the water, so Teapot and I swim across alone, back to where I'd left my boots. Once there, I take my socks off again, wring them out, and put them back on. Then, clutching willow branches to keep from slipping, I climb the steep side to the flat top of the levee.

What I'd wished for—to see cars whizzing past on a distant Tamiami Trail—isn't to be. There's only the glaringly white levee stretching endlessly before me, with a humid mist rising as the sun dries the hard-packed surface.

I'd hoped that once on the dry ground, I'd be able to let my feet dry out, but my soles are too raw and tender to walk barefoot across the sharp seashells and gravel. They are too raw, even, for the rubber boots without the damp socks. With Teapot in my bandana, it feels like I'm crossing hot coals. I bend my knees to absorb some of the pain, but it doesn't help.

I'm so focused on the pain of walking that I hear the rattled warning before I see the snake, even though it lies just two yards ahead of me in the middle of the levee. It coils and rings its tail again.

"There's a little rattlesnake right in front of me," I call to Andy. He's walking nearly parallel to me, but in the knee-deep water on the saw-grass prairie side of the canal.

"Find a stick and poke it out of the way."

I look around. "There's nothing like that here."

"Can't you walk around him?"

"He's right in the middle."

"The levee's gotta be ten feet wide."

"That's not wide enough."

There's probably a four-foot clearance on either side of the snake, but it looks like four inches to me. Teapot squirms in the bandana, wanting out since I'm not moving. Andy is wearing the backpack, which would have been a safer place to carry her.

"I need the pack—for Teapot."

Andy looks across at me. "I can't throw it that far."

"Well, try." I back away from the snake, then cross to the edge of the levee.

Andy takes it off, swings his arm in a couple of wide circles... "Wait!" I scream as he launches the pack. I watch it soar across the water to land among the willows about three feet shy of where I'm standing.

"The camera," he says. "I forgot the camera."

"So did I. I hope the willows cushioned it."

Holding onto branches as I go, I lower myself down the slope until I can reach the pack, snag it, and climb back up. I unzip the bottom compartment and take out the Leica. The body seems okay, but the barrel of the lens is badly dented. *I'm so sorry, Daddy.*

"Did it break?" Andy's standing with his hands on his hips.

"The lens doesn't look too good."

"I'm sorry."

"Not your fault."

The snake hasn't moved except to relax its coils, which it tightens again when it sees me, or smells me or whatever it does.

I put Teapot in the top of the pack, then break off a willow branch, but it's too wispy and not nearly long enough. Most of the shells and gravel are ground too fine, but at the edges of the levee there are a few larger chunks. I find one that isn't too big to hurt the snake if I actually hit it, throw it, and miss completely.

"That does it." I scoop up a handful of shells, sand, and gravel and rain that down on the snake.

It lifts its head and rings its tail. I throw another fistful. The snake strikes, fangs exposed.

Though it's too far away to actually bite me, I leap back when it strikes. The pain that shoots up both my legs drops me to my knees. I fall forward, catch myself with my hands, then scramble backwards away from where the snake was when I fell. I stop only when I realize that it has disappeared into the willows at the side of the levee.

I look at Andy, ready to let him know I'm all right, only to find he's walked on ahead.

"I'm okay," I shout.

My knees are covered with a powdery white dust, through which I'm bleeding from a dozen cuts. The heels of my hands look the same, cut, scraped, and bloody. I sit picking shell fragments out of my knees and crying.

Andy must have glanced back and seen me sitting there because he shouts, "Are you okay?"

"I fell." I wonder what he would have done if the snake had bitten me. It wasn't like he could swim over or run for help.

I finally get to my feet and start my limpy, gimpy way along the levee. I've only gone a dozen yards or so when I see something glinting in the sun. I shield my eyes. Whatever it is flicks like someone sending a signal, not like the wings of the airplanes when they bank to turn. Besides, it's closer than any of the planes, and it's coming from a tree island.

Andy's ahead of me again. He turns when I shout his name.

"What?"

"I don't know. I see something in those trees over there."

Whatever it is isn't moving. The flashing is caused by the wind moving tree branches.

"What is it?"

"I don't know. It's shiny."

He looks where I'm pointing, then shrugs. "I don't see anything."

"Well, I'm higher than you are."

He loses interest and trudges on.

I begin to move again, too, but the light keeps drawing my eye. "Do they ever use tin for the roofs of the cabins?"

Andy's plodding along, but when I say that his head snaps up. "It's a camp," he shouts. "Where? Where is it?"

I point a little south and west of him.

"Come on." He begins to run.

"Wait for me," I call.

He's running, plowing the air with his elbows held like Teapot's nubby wings, twisting from side to side with each step.

"Andy!" I shout. "Don't leave me—" I say to myself.

When I can no longer tell he's a human, I sit down. I'll wait for him to come back or for the searchers to find me. My T-shirt is yellow. Surely, they'll be able to see me when they get a little closer. I take the backpack off, hug it to my chest, and lie back. If I think school is a lonely place, look at me now. Tears run from my eyes into my ears.

19

I don't know how long I lie there before I begin to hear Teapot peeping. "Shhh." I pat the pack. It's hot to the touch. "Oh, my God." I sit up. The dark maroon pack has been soaking up the sun and cooking Teapot. When I unzip the top, she's lying with her neck stretched out and her beak open. Her sides heave.

I get my feet under me, only to crumple from the pain. I look frantically for a break in the cattails and willows where I can get down to the water. "Don't die. Please don't die." I fan her, then struggle to stand again.

I keep fanning her as I limp along the levee, looking for a path to the water. A few yards down I find a spot where the willows are sparse. Almost the second I start down the steep, gravelly bank my feet go out from under me. I know the instant before I hit the ground that if I try to break my fall, I'll have to drop Teapot. I go with the momentum of my body, land on my left shoulder, and slide all the way to the water's edge on my bare arm.

The pain is excruciating. I lie there groaning. My left arm is twisted behind my back and, since I've come to a stop on my side, my full weight is on top of it. It feels broken. I lift my head and look at Teapot lying in the open pack, which I've somehow managed to keep balanced in my right hand. I put it down in the shade of the willow that's behind me. Her breathing is shallow.

I try to sit up without using my left hand, but can't get leverage. I reach with my right, grab a willow branch, and pull myself up to a sitting position. That's when I hear the now too-familiar rattle.

The air leaves my lungs in a gasp. I hold perfectly still for a moment before slowly turning just my eyes. I don't see it and am hoping it has slipped away when the dead leaves at the base of the willow, whose branch I still hold, move. It's among them—two feet away—watching me, its tongue flicking in and out.

I can't move or think what to do. Andy is gone. Even if he comes back, I'm not where I was when he ran off. I'm in dense willows, which will make it hard for anyone to spot me. If the snake strikes, there won't be anything he or anyone else can do.

The rush of blood pumping through my body sounds like a train in my ears. I imagine my skeleton being found by a fisherman one day, mine and Teapot's, side by side.

The muscle in my right arm trembles from holding the willow branch.

If I'm going to die here, let's get it over with. I squeeze my eyes shut and let go. I hear the branch whoosh back into place and cringe, expecting to feel fangs pierce my arm. When nothing happens, I take a deep breath and open my eyes. The snake is just where it had been, still tasting the air between us. "Go away," I whisper. "Please, please, please, go away."

I sit there, letting the minutes seep by. My body aches and my muscles begin to stiffen. The blood on my knees dries and turns black. I watch the snake while I rotate my left shoulder and, though it hurts terribly, it moves and my arm seems to be okay, just badly scraped and bloody. The breeze dies and mosquitoes begin to whine, land, and take advantage of the exposed blood. I watch their abdomens swell.

Teapot's breathing is almost normal, but she's still unconscious. The snake looks pretty relaxed, and it occurs to me that it might have gone to sleep. I want to lie down, too—put my head back and rest for a while. And I'm thirsty—terribly thirsty. I close my eyes and try to think about what it will be like when I get home. I can almost smell the line-dried, sunshiny scent of the sheets that will be on my bed.

Fresh rustling in the leaves startles me. I glance at the snake. It's exactly as it had been. I look a little higher up the slope. A little mouse with huge ears moves toward me, sniffing and snuffling among the grasses and dead leaves beneath the willows.

For the longest time, the snake's tongue has not appeared, which was the reason I thought it may have gone to sleep, but now its head turns ever so slightly in the direction of the mouse and its tongue slides out—the forked tip flicks the air.

My heart aches for the little mouse, so oblivious to its fate. "Shoo," I say, and the mouse freezes. The snake is deaf, but the mouse isn't. "Scram," I say.

It scurries into a little tunnel of grasses. The snake straightens and begins to slide after it. When it, too, disappears, I put the pack with Teapot on my lap and scoot into the water on my butt. Keeping an eye on where the snake has gone, I gently lift Teapot and hold her so only her feet are in the cool water. Her lolling head rests on my thumb.

Long minutes pass before she blinks and opens her eyes. When she does, I tip her so she can drink, then carefully put her in the water. Though she seems sluggish, she stays upright and bobs against the shore.

I stare at the far side of the canal. *To hell with you, Andy. I'll find the camp without you.* I take my boots off. Thank heavens it's not my right arm that is too sore to lift. I throw first one boot, then the other, as hard as I can, then slide into the water and swim to meet them.

I'd done pretty well. They've landed near each other and bump as they float back toward me. I swim as quickly as the pain in my shoulder will allow, checking to make sure Teapot follows.

I catch the first boot and pitch it out of the canal. I hear the splash of it landing in the shallow water on the other side of the berm. The second one gets away from me and I have to chase it down. Once I catch it, my arm hurts too much to swim back against the current, so I pull out on the boulders where I am, put a hand under Teapot and lift her over the edge, then follow on scraped hands and knees.

From this side, which is probably ten feet lower than the levee, I can't see the roof of the camp, and have no idea where Andy is. Still, I cup my hands around my mouth and shout his name.

Nothing. Just the whispering grasses and a hawk calling as it makes slow circles high above me.

I sit in the shallow water for a few minutes, then put the one boot on, get up, and limp back up the side of the canal until I find the other one.

"We're on our own," I tell Teapot. I take a deep breath and squint at the sun. If I keep it on my face, I'll be headed pretty much southwest.

Since the saw grass here is sparse and grows low, I leave Teapot out to let her swim along beside me, but she gets busy eating so I pick her up and put her in the sling so she can see out.

By the angle of the sun, I guess it must be after four. I'm trying not to think about what will happen if I'm not headed in exactly the right direction. Darkness will come, and I'll be out here alone. If a whole squad of search planes can't find us, how will we ever find each other again? *Is Andy even looking for me?* It doesn't matter. I'll find him— and the cabin.

Each time I come to anything I can stand on—a rock outcropping, a small tree, some matted vegetation—I step up and try to glimpse the roof of the cabin. When I come to a good size pond-apple tree, I climb it, shade my eyes and search the horizon, but the sun is all wrong now—too low. There are a couple tree islands a half-mile or so ahead, but is either the right one? I glance behind me to see where to put my foot before climbing down when out of the corner of my eye I see a flash. There it is. The closer of the two islands. "We're headed the right way," I tell Teapot.

One of the search planes combs the horizon near where I think we started from. Due west and a little north. The orange Coast Guard helicopter is a bit closer and directly north of me. For the heck of it, I wave, even though it's so far away I can't hear its engine.

It takes me nearly an hour to reach a point where I can actually see the camp through the trees. The closer I get, the harder it is to get my legs to work. My dad likes old movies, and I remember seeing more than one where a man who's dying of thirst in the desert sees a water oasis. He crawls and drags himself toward it, not knowing until it's too late that it's a mirage, just sun shimmering on sand. I keep my eyes locked on the cabin, afraid that if I look away, it will vanish like Andy's fishermen. Each step is an effort in slow motion. When I finally reach the open water of the dredged pond that separates me from the rickety dock, dry land, and the cabin, my legs are like lead.

As close as I am, I can't move another inch. I sit down in the shallow water and let Teapot out of the sling. Won't it be something if the searchers, days from now, found me still here, ten yards from the likelihood of food? I lie back in the water and close my eyes.

I don't know how long I lie there; it's impossible to care. Only Teapot swimming over, climbing onto my chest and snuggling up next to my chin brings me back. I open my eyes. The sky is pink above my head, red and orange in the west. I put Teapot back in the water, sit up, and pull off my boots. I fling them across the pond, swim slowly over, and belly out onto the grass.

When I try to get up, my legs tremble like my arm muscles sometimes do after I carry something heavy. I walk the plank dock to the front of the cabin. It's dark inside, but by the dim light coming through the screen door I see Andy curled on the floor, moaning and holding his stomach. He's surrounded by a litter of empty cans: peaches, pears and pineapples. If he hears me enter, he doesn't look up. I walk over and stand dripping beside him. If it wasn't for the pain in my feet, I'd kick him. I look instead to see if there is anything he hasn't eaten.

There are a few cubes left in the bottom of the can of pineapple. Since Andy has pulled every drawer open looking for the can opener, I don't have to search for a fork. I finish the pineapple, closing my eyes to relish the sweetness, then drink the juice.

The cabin is much nicer than the one we left, which isn't saying a lot. It's set up the same, with bunk beds, and windows with rusty metal rods for braces rather than broomsticks. When I pop one open, Teapot chases down and eats a cockroach, then another that has been startled by the addition of light.

The sink is newer, though not cleaner. There are a few more cans of food on the plank shelves along with a Coleman stove. I lift the fabric skirt someone made to cover the pipes under the sink. There is a can of Raid, a trap with the fur-covered skeleton of a mouse caught by the neck, a tin of saltines, and a rusting propane tank, which is light but not empty.

Though the tin hasn't kept the saltines fresh, they taste wonderful. I break some up and scatter them for Teapot, then inspect a can of Hormel chili. It doesn't look swollen, although when I wipe the dust off with the hem of my wet shirt, the expiration date is three years ago. I get the opener from the floor beside Andy, open the can, and sniff it. *Smells okay.*

After studying the stove for a minute or so, I figure out how to attach the propane tank to it. I find waterproof matches in a drawer and after a few tries get the Coleman lit. I empty the chili into a saucepan that I've wiped clean with my shirt. In no time, the room fills with the smell of bubbling hot chili.

I take two spoons from the drawer by the sink and go to sit on the floor with Andy.

He's been watching me. "What happened to your arm?"

"I slid down the side of the levee and landed next to a pygmy rattlesnake." I should know by now, guilt doesn't work very well on Andy.

"I'm sorry," he says. Nothing else.

I look at him for a moment then shrug. "It doesn't matter."

"I couldn't think of anything except getting something to eat."

I hand him a spoon. "Want some chili?"

"My stomach's killing me."

Serves you right.

Teapot comes over and stands on her tiptoes and stretches her neck, trying to see what I'm eating. I break up more crackers for her and crumble some into the chili. When I've eaten enough to stop the pain in my stomach, I hold the pot out to Andy.

He shakes his head.

I eat slowly until I finish it all and push the pot away.

Andy crosses his arms over his stomach, rolls back into a ball on the floor, and moans. "I think some of that fruit was bad."

"You can't go without food for three days, then stuff yourself." Even my stomach starts to hurt again, but it's from the shock of food, not the empty ache I've felt for days.

The bedding is filthy, so I lie down on the floor beside Andy. I stare at the water stain on the plywood ceiling for a moment, then turn, put my arm across his shoulder, and fall instantly to sleep.

When I wake the first time, it's dark. Andy's on his back, snoring, one arm flung out to his side, the other bent behind his head for a pillow. My last thought before I drift off again is how much more comfortable this is than a tree limb.

The next time I wake it's because Andy's tickling my arm. "What?"

He doesn't answer.

I feel it again and open my eyes. The cabin's pitch black, and I have to pee. *The moon should be up soon.* I decide to wait until then to go outside. I roll toward Andy and hear something crunch under my right hip. *Teapot!* I sit up. Something's crawling on my leg. I brush it away, but feel another on my neck, then another on my arm. Bugs. Lots of them. I scramble to my feet. It's like being blind. I can't see what's on me or make out any shapes in the room. Whatever they are, they're climbing my legs. I scream and dance in place, knocking them away with my hands.

"What?" Andy says.

"Something's crawling on me."

"Jesus. Me, too." It's so totally dark in the cabin that I only know he's gotten up because he grunts from the effort. I hear popping sounds as he feels his way to the sink where I left the matches.

"Be careful," I cry. "I don't know where Teapot is."

I hear his hand hit and knock the matchbox to the floor.

"Hurry, please." As fast as I knock a few away, I feel others land on me. They are in my hair. My back is covered with them. One flies and lands on my cheek.

"Get outside," Andy says. From the location of his voice, he's on his knees trying to find the matchbox.

"I don't know where the door is."

His hand hits the box. He tears it open, scattering the matches, but finds at least one because he strikes it. In the momentary burst of light, before the match fizzles and goes out, I see roaches. Roaches everywhere.

Andy strikes another match. Roaches on the walls, on the floor, in the chili pot, a layer of them covering the screened part of the door, blocking all light. "Teapot," I cry. "Where are you?"

The match goes out, but not before Andy reaches the front door. When he touches it the screen seems to crack like plaster as the roaches fly into the room. Moonlight splashes in and illuminates the rippling mass of insects cascading over the counter top and up the walls. I see Teapot run from beneath a bunk, headed for the door.

My bare feet squish roaches as I cross the room, open the door, and flee outside with Teapot. I run with my knees bent to absorb the shocking pain in my feet, cross the yard, and plunge into the pond with Andy.

The taste of chili rises and burns my throat.

. . .

We sleep side by side on the grass at the water's edge. It's nearly dawn when I wake to Andy's racket in the cabin. I tilt my head back. "What are you doing?"

"Cleaning up a little."

He's sweeping the empty cans toward the door.

"Are there still roaches in there?"

"Palmetto bugs. No. They're gone. I put the chili pot on the step, will you wash it out?"

"Yeah." I get up. "Don't come out 'til I tell you, okay? I've got to pee."

Teapot stands, stretches one leg then the other, and pads after me to the cabin, then back to the water. "Go eat," I tell her. I fill the pot with water to soak off the dried chili, then go behind the croton hedge to pee. I'm just pulling my pants up when I hear the *whop, whop, whop* of rotary blades. I step out from behind the hedge as the helicopter's belly number goes right over my head. I can't see the pilot and know he hasn't seen me.

I run into the cabin and grab my backpack. Andy and I try to get back out at the same time, jamming the doorway.

He pushes through, runs down to the water, plunges in and wades to the middle where it's the most open.

I unzip the bottom of the pack and dump the contents onto the grass. A bit of morning sun shines through the trees in splinters of light. I find my mirror and flick my wrist until I catch the light, then reflect it toward the helicopter. It's too late. The bright white circle deflects off the tail of the chopper. I drop my arm. What difference does it make? We'll walk back to the levee this morning and be out by afternoon. Still, when I squat to put everything back into the pack, tears roll down my cheeks.

DAY FIVE

20

Knowing how close we are makes it harder to think about getting into the water again. I feel like I've used up all my luck. I look at my wrecked feet, then at my legs, which are covered with bites and crisscrossed with saw-grass cuts. I touch my swollen, lumpy cheek, wet with the tears I can't control. "Look back, please," I say to the departing helicopter.

It has banked a little to the right, enough for me to see the copilot's profile. I flick the mirror again. The little circle of light hits his right earphone. Before I have time to wonder if maybe, out of the corner of his eye, he's seen it, he turns and shields his eyes.

I wave.

Andy's wading back toward shore. When he realizes the helicopter is returning, he begins to shout and wave his arms. "We're here," he hollers. "We're here."

I flash the mirror across his face, smile and drop it into the pack.

The sound of the helicopter frightens Teapot, who flees into the cattails at the edge of the pond. Calling her is pointless. The noise of the helicopter drowns out everything. I'll have to go after her.

Overnight the socks have dried black and as stiff as cardboard. I hunker at the edge of the pond and float them in the water, trying to soften them up. It hurts just thinking about putting them on again—ever. I toss them on the shore, rinse, and gingerly slip my feet into the remains of my boots. It feels as if I'm pouring alcohol on open wounds. I squeeze my eyes shut against the pain.

Andy reaches shore. "Where are you going?" he shouts over the roar of the helicopter.

"Teapot's in the cattails."

He glances that direction. "I don't see her," he hollers.

I look at him, then step off into the water.

He catches my arm. "I'll get her."

The helicopter comes in and hovers near the end of the dock, about the only spot open enough for the blades to clear the treetops.

I watch Andy wade into the wildly blowing cattails.

The copilot opens the side door of the helicopter and prepares to drop a sling-like chair, which is attached to the end of a cable. I hold up one finger, then point to my wrist where a watch would be. A moment later Andy breaks out of the cattails with his big hands wrapped gently around Teapot.

I take her from him, zip her into the top of the pack, then put it on backwards so I can hold it against my chest. The copilot slowly lowers the chair, at the same time signaling the pilot as he maneuvers the helicopter until it's almost directly above my head. The downdraft from the rotating blades nearly knocks me off my feet as I try to catch the chair and hold it still enough to get into. Andy comes up behind me and, after two tries, catches and holds it for me. Almost immediately I feel my feet leave the dock.

When I'm dangling just outside the door of the helicopter, the copilot reaches, grabs the cable, and pulls me and the chair inside.

"I'm Joe. Nice to see you," he yells over the *whop, whop* of the blades.

"Sarah, and ditto." I shake his hand. Tears swim in my eyes.

Joe lowers the chair to Andy, and while he reels him in, I look out at the landscape we've crossed. Miles and miles of saw grass, tree islands, and the sparkling patches of nearly open water. I remember how I felt on the observation tower four days ago. How ugly and desolate I thought it was—nothing but a hideous sameness. Now from the helicopter I can see the white ribbon of the levee and the trail that I cut across to the camp, and Andy's path, less direct than mine. I wonder how long it will take for those traces to disappear. I look down to smile at Andy and see the chili pot and Andy's socks by the water's edge.

Maybe I can find out who owns this camp and call to tell them I hadn't meant to leave those dirty things for them.

. . .

The helicopter ride back to the Tamiami Trail is thrilling. In spite of how thankful I am to be headed home, I can't take my eyes off the view from up here. I try to pick out the camp where the airboat sank, but if I'm seeing it, it's indistinguishable from any other tree island. Still, I feel ownership, somehow. Bits and pieces of me are down there, skin and heart. Nothing can ever take that away.

The chopper veers off a direct course to the Trail and over an airboat driven by a single Miccosukee Indian. He's the same one I'd seen skim by the windows of the restaurant that first day. The copilot writes something on a piece of paper and puts it inside a red-and-yellow container that looks like a big fishing bobber. When the Indian stops his airboat, the copilot drops the message to him, then the pilot banks toward the Trail.

"He's been searching since Sunday," he shouts. "I was letting him know we've got you."

His must have been the lone airboat we heard after we left the dead tree with the coffeepot.

There are two ambulances parked parallel to Andy's truck and two police cars pulled lengthwise across the road to block traffic so the helicopter can land. Near the top of the boat ramp, I see my parents. My father is standing by the trunk of our old car, shielding his eyes against the morning sun. Mom is standing beside him, her hands clutching his arm, her forehead against his shoulder. A wave of pity for them both, but especially my mother, sweeps over me. *She thought I was dead.*

"Those are my parents," I yell in Andy's ear. "Do you see yours?"

"That's my father's truck. I don't see Mom," he yells back.

As badly as I feel for my parents, tears come when I see Mr. Vickers's red head in the crowd.

The helicopter puts down in the middle of the road and paramedics run toward it with stretchers. When the copilot lifts me and hands me off to one of them, the crowd that has gathered begins to applaud and cheer.

"I'm okay," I tell him when he puts me on the stretcher. "My feet hurt, but I'm fine. Really." All this fuss is kind of embarrassing.

I watch Andy let the copilot help him from the helicopter. When he spots his father coming, he hops on the other stretcher and lies down. I guess he figures he's safer going to the hospital than home with his dad.

The police let my parents duck under the yellow crime-scene ribbon. I bite my lip. "I'm so sorry," I say when Dad puts his arms around me. He smells like he always does—of tar and sweat and Old Spice.

"Nothing matters. You're safe."

"I'm so sorry, Mom." I hug her, but when I try to draw away, Mom holds on. It reminds me of Andy after he kicked the snake away.

My mom's not a very affectionate person. "I'm okay, Mom. Really."

Still she holds on.

"Let her lie down, honey," Daddy says. "She's okay."

"I thought you were dead," Mom says. She's crushing my hand in hers as they wheel the gurney to the ambulance. My mother looks like she's a hundred.

"I'm really sorry, Momma." They're just about to fold the legs under and slide me into the ambulance, when I see Mr. Vickers standing behind the yellow ribbon.

"Wait." I sit up.

My father looks where I'm looking. "That man is totally irresponsible," he says. "He deserves to be fired."

"No he doesn't. It was my fault. I lied to him." I swing my legs off the gurney and hop off. Daddy grabs my arm to keep me from falling when my legs buckle.

"What are you doing?" He puts his hands in my armpits and tries to lift me back onto the stretcher.

"I have an apology to make." I limp down the grassy side of the road.

"I'm so glad you're okay," Mr. Vickers says when I put my arms around him and my head against his chest.

"I'm sorry I made you worry." I look up at him. "Do you remember how you said you wanted us to learn to love this place?"

He nods.

"Well, I do. It's beautiful. Just like you said. Scary but beautiful."

"Maybe you'll tell us all about it when you come back to school."

"I have to do a report?" I try to look astonished, then smile.

The Miccosukee from the airboat comes toward us. "I thought you'd like to have this," he says and hands me the bobber they dropped to him from the helicopter.

"Thank you. And thank you for looking for us."

"You should be very proud of yourselves. I've found 'em alive and dead out there, but not many come out healthy. Lack of food, fear, and the mosquitoes have driven grown men crazy."

After the Indian pats my shoulder and walks away, I open the bobber, take out the rolled-up note, and uncurl it: *Lost souls on board*.

Nothing I've ever read could make me feel more alive.

They've put Andy in the other ambulance. His father is standing by the open door with his hands on his hips, watching my father march toward him. I'm afraid of what they might say to each other. "Daddy," I call, but he doesn't turn. I limp toward them.

"... mad at you for getting my daughter into this," Dad's saying when I come up beside him.

"I'm sure your daughter is as much to blame as my . . ."

"Shut up, Dad," Andy says.

My father doesn't even acknowledge Andy's father. ". . . but I want to thank you for getting her out."

"Sir, I didn't. She . . ."

I interrupt. "Andy saved me, Dad. He was amazing."

I turn to Mr. Malone. "I'm Sarah, sir, and I'm very sorry." I put my hand out.

He looks at me, his eyes blue ice. I drop the offer of my hand.

My father steps between us and stares down at Andy's father.

I wonder how many times he's held his resentment wadded in his stomach instead of in the fists that are knotted at his sides.

"It's okay, Daddy." I look at Andy's father. "Your son saved my life, and I saved his, Mr. Malone. Gave him mouth-to-mouth." I smile.

The ambulance driver steps forward, puts a hand against Mr. Malone's chest to move him back so he can close the doors.

"Wait, please." I touch the driver's arm.

I haven't let go of my backpack, and no one seems to have noticed the occasional peep coming from the top portion. I unzip the bottom half and take out the Swiss Army knife. "I don't think my brother will mind if you have this." I hand it to Andy. "I'll save up and buy him a new one."

"I'm nothing like him, Sarah." He's referring to his father.

"Don't you think I know that?"

He holds the knife in his palm then closes his fist around it. "Thank you."

I lean and hug him. "I'll write to you," I whisper, then back away. The driver shuts the second door.

Andy's father watches, tight-jawed, turns and marches toward his truck. The front license tag is also a Confederate flag.

My dad puts his arm around my shoulders and kisses my forehead.

The ambulance turns on its siren and pulls out onto the highway.

"Where are they taking him?"

"Naples, I think." Dad scoops me up like he used to do when I was little and carries me toward the other ambulance.

I put my head against his chest. "Poor Andy. His dad's a bigger jerk than I'd imagined."

"Yeah. I've known a million of them."

"Was his mother here?"

"She only left an hour ago. Nice woman. And that teacher of yours has driven out here every day."

"I don't want you causing him any trouble, Dad. It was totally my fault. I didn't want to go on the field trip 'cause I thought all the other girls hated me. It was all just an accident."

"What did happen?"

"I don't suppose they found the airboat."

"Isn't it where they found you?"

I smile. "Not even close. Andy forgot to put the stern plug in after he washed it. We got about ten miles out, stopped at a hunting camp to picnic, and it sank."

My father puts me on the stretcher. "You mean to tell me you weren't where they found you the whole time?

"We just got there yesterday afternoon."

"Why didn't you stay where the airboat sank?"

"We couldn't. Andy said nobody would find us there. We hiked the ten miles to the levee, then to the camp because we thought there would be food there. And there was." I pull off a boot.

My father gasps.

"Ten miles. Three days. No food or water?" He can't take his eyes off my feet.

"Andy dug scratch wells, so we had clean water, and we chewed on pieces of his belt to keep from feeling so hungry..." The backpack is on my stomach. I unzip the top portion. "And this is Teapot." My duckling pops her head out.

Dad laughs.

"We ... I ran over her brother with the boat and scared the mother duck off, so we brought her out with us."

A camera flash goes off.

The next morning, on the front page of the *Miami Herald*, is a picture of me lying on the stretcher, smiling at Dad whose face registers shock as Teapot scrambles from the backpack to snuggle under my chin. The headline reads: *Two Students Lost in the Everglades Found Alive.* The story followed: "Sarah Emerson, a Glades Academy student, missing in the Everglades since Saturday, was found alive late yesterday afternoon. Emerson, Andrew Malone, of Naples, and a baby mallard duck were found unharmed . . ."

. . .

By Wednesday morning, I have a huge bouquet of flowers from Mr. Vickers in my hospital room and two stuffed animals, a yellow duckling and an alligator. A few cards arrive in the afternoon mail, and those, to my surprise, are mostly from the kids who'd been on the field trip—Philip, Raymond, and the two Amandas. All were signed, *your friend*. Mr. Vickers must have forced them to write.

Andy calls first thing Wednesday morning. "How's it going?"

"Okay. How about you?"

"I'm home already. When are you getting out?"

"Tomorrow or Friday. The blisters on my feet got infected. Did you get in a lot of trouble?"

"I don't think they've decided yet. What was cool is my mother cried when she saw me, and Dad's bragging about me to all his cronies out here. I guess that's good."

"I'm glad, Andy."

"I'm still really sorry about what happened, you know?"

"You don't have to be. After this I feel like I can do anything. We walked out of the Everglades. What could possibly be tougher than that?"

"Getting my father to let me out of our front yard ever again."

I laugh.

"Whatcha going to do with Teapot?"

The question stings, but I shrug my hospital-gowned shoulders. "She's at home in my bathtub right now." I don't want to think about what will become of Teapot. "My parents are having some people over for a little welcome home party on Saturday, can you come?"

Nothing. Only silence.

"Andy?"

"My father would never let me."

"Don't ask him. Ask your mother."

"I will, but don't count on it."

"I'll try not to, but I've kind of gotten in the habit of counting on you."

There's only the sound of his breathing for a moment, then he says, "And me on you."

I'm holding the bobber the Miccosukee gave me and staring at the pattern in the tile ceiling when my mom comes in a few minutes later. She puts an overnight case on the end of the bed, so close to one of my sore feet that I flinch.

"That poor little duck keeps peeping for you," she says.

I close my eyes.

. . .

When I get home on Friday morning, I go straight to my bathroom and open the shower curtain. Teapot launches herself out of the disgusting looking litter-box pool Mom put on the floor of the tub and tries to pop out and over the side of the tub. I catch her and hold her under my chin. The inside of the bathtub looks as if an avocado has exploded and aged to a golden brown.

I kiss her head while Teapot runs her bill through my hair, making peaceful little hiccuppy noises. Lewis, our dog, snorts and snuffles, his nose pressed to the crack beneath the door.

I wipe the tub out with toilet paper, flush the wads of seed, then rinse the litter box and run the shower to wash the tub. I put Teapot back in her clean pool, but when I slide the shower curtain closed, Teapot flings herself against it. Lewis starts to bark.

"Stop it." I whack the door with my palm. What *am* I going to do with Teapot?

21

"What are your plans for that duck?" Mom asks when I limp into the kitchen after cleaning the tub.

"I don't have any."

"Maybe your dad can build it a little pen and we can keep it in the yard."

I remember Andy's pet snake and his purple gallinule. I want that kind of freedom for Teapot. "I need time to think this through, okay?"

"I'm sorry. You're right, but you have to decide pretty soon. It's driving the dog—"

On cue, Lewis begins to bark again.

"Lewis," I shout. "Shut up."

"I told her she has to decide what to do with the poor little thing before the dog digs under the door," Mom says, when Dad comes into the kitchen.

"Actually, I just settled that," he says.

Since getting back, I'm always either hungry or, if I've just eaten, thinking about what I'd like to eat next. I turn from staring into the refrigerator. "What do you mean?"

"I did a roofing job at Macaw World a few months ago. I called the owner, and he agreed to give Teapot a home. She can live on the flamingo pond."

I stare at him. I'm not prepared for this. In fact, deep down, I'm not ready to accept that I really have to give her up and am still trying to think of a way to keep her. "That . . . that's wonderful, Dad," I say, but my expression must have given away how I feel because Mom takes my hand and squeezes it.

"I've got something else for you." He opens the Publix grocery bag he's carrying.

I try to imagine the world's largest avocado, which he will fill with his special crab salad. Instead he has an envelope of photographs.

"I'm sorry about breaking your camera lens, Dad."

"Do you think that matters? Besides, it's in the shop, and they said they can fix it. One tough camera; one tough photographer." He hands me the envelope.

I open the envelope and take out the five prints. The top picture is of the AABCs. They look like a row of starlets in their perfect little outfits and their perfect hair and teeth, gaudied up like clones of each other. It dawns on me that in a year or two I won't remember who was who. They will be what they always were, unimportant in my life. I lay the picture down on the counter in front of the toaster.

The second one is mostly a blur of muddy water and wings, but I can still see the alligator's jaws have snapped shut on the heron's legs, and the fish is still skewered on the heron's bill. I look at Mom, then at Dad; they are standing on either side of me.

"An action shot of the food chain," Dad says.

"I took this picture from a sixty-five foot tower. How could I have ever imagined that by the next morning I would no longer be at the top of that chain, but somewhere in the middle?"

The next is a wonderful picture of Andy, handsome and smiling at the camera. I don't know if it's the old Dodge truck behind him and the Pan Am flight bag he's carrying, but he looks as if he's from a different time.

"That's a nice picture of you," Mom says of the next one.

I feel struck by lightning. I'm smiling at the camera, too, just like the Barbies, except of course, I'm the black one. My makeup is perfect, my teeth are white, my lips and fingernails are red, and I'm wearing an *outfit*—matched as well as I could match old shorts, a T-shirt, the bandana and my boots. The difference is my eyes are dull and my shoulders are humped up around my ears. I'm looking at a girl who had retreated into herself.

The Leica focuses differently from the digital cameras the other kids had. When the two images in the viewfinder merge, the camera reads how far the photographer is from the subject. For a moment I consider tearing up the picture of me, but decide I will keep it as a reminder of how far away I am from that girl perched on the seat of the airboat. She and the boat lie forever in the mud at the bottom of a pond.

The last picture is of the python killing the alligator. Andy's a blur in the foreground, but the life-and-death struggle behind him is sharp and clear.

"God," Dad says.

Mom presses a hand to her chest. "I'd have died right there of a heart attack," she says.

. . .

On the next Saturday, Dad and I drive south out of Coconut Grove to Macaw World, which is on Red Road. I'd been there once when my cousin from Alabama visited, but that was when I was eight. I didn't remember anything about it except a cockatoo on roller skates.

If Dad didn't have a connection with the owner, they would never have agreed to take Teapot. A mallard is neither exotic nor a draw for the tourist dollar.

Teapot paces the interior of the box I hold in my lap. She's doubled in size over this last week. Her breast and belly are losing their downy yellow feathers, replaced instead by tightly packed, waterproof adult ones. Her wings are still nubs, but stubby little pinfeathers, encased in gunmetal gray shafts, have begun to appear.

If I thought walking out of the Everglades was the hardest thing I'd ever have to do, I was wrong. That was physical. Giving Teapot up makes me feel as if my heart is going to break. I've cried myself dry over the last few days, and my parents don't know how to make this easier. Even now, Dad and I are driving there in silence. I'm glad. I just want to think about Andy, Teapot, and the Everglades.

"Have you heard from Andy?" Dad's looking at me, his face creased with concern.

It startles me that he should ask just when I was thinking about him. "Yes. A couple of phone calls and a few e-mails from a computer at his school. He's fine. On restriction until he can vote, but fine."

"Nice boy, but that duck's got a better chance of making something of himself than Andy does, poor kid."

"What makes you say that?" My tone is snappy.

"Don't get me wrong, I'm not wishing failure on him. I just don't think he has the initiative to overcome where he lives and his father."

I turn and stare out the window. "He knows nearly everything about the Everglades."

"That will only help him if he sinks another boat."

"He got me out in one piece."

Out of the corner of my eye, I see Dad glance at me. "You know what I think?"

"No." I'm mad at him for talking about Andy like that, and for finding a place for Teapot. I want him to shut up.

"I think that if he'd broken his leg, or got bitten by that moccasin, you would have walked out on your own."

"No way. I was scared of everything that moved out there."

"You weren't by the time you got out, were you?"

I shrug. "I don't know. I guess I finally realized I was scaring them more than they were scaring me."

"That's not the half of it. You've got guts, Sarah."

"I sure didn't start out with any. Maybe I got them from a mosquito bite." I try to smile. "You know," I say after a minute. "We both did what we had to do to get out, and we did it by tapping into what we were each good at. We were a team."

I think again about the picture of Andy that I took. It's in a little frame by my computer. I figured out why he looks like he's from a different era. He has a kind face like Mr. Vickers. Not many of us do anymore.

Teapot's attempting to leap out of the box through the gap in the lid. I can feel her leave the bottom, fall, struggle to her feet and leap again. It reminds me of how I pushed myself to keep going. I wonder if Dad's right. Did I always have what it took to get out of there, or does it seem that way because I made it? I try to think back on how many times I said, "I can't," yet every time I could, and I did. Maybe I've always underestimated myself because other people saw me as black and a girl, and made all kinds of assumptions about who I was and what I was capable of. I don't see myself through their eyes anymore. I see myself through my own.

I look at my dad's profile. "I made the wrong choice to go in the airboat with Andy," I say, "but I'm glad it happened. It's awesome out there, Dad, and it changed me."

Each time Teapot hears my voice, she tries harder to get out.

"How so?" Dad says.

"You and Mom tried to load me with self-confidence, but when I was at Tucker, I never had to face competition or disappointment or disapproval. At Glades no one thinks I'm special—except maybe Mr. Vickers. And none of the kids want anything to do with me. Andy's just the opposite of me. He's had no one to tell him that he's smart or brave or can accomplish anything he sets out to do. I've had all kinds of support from you and Mom, he's had none, yet he rose to the challenge of getting us out of there. He lived up to what I expected of him.

"I've wondered for days why he didn't tell me he couldn't swim. At first I thought it was stupid of him, but now I think it was because he felt obligated to save me—like he could will himself to swim. If he was ever afraid, he never let it show. All day, every day, he fought down the pain he must have felt to protect me. So you're wrong about him. We both came out changed from the way we went in." I stop and think of the minnows eating the skin

I washed out of my socks. "I'm brand new." I open the box and lift Teapot out. "And Andy is my best friend."

Dad takes his foot off the gas and steers to the side of the road into the parking lot of a fruit stand.

"You can't imagine what we went through. We thought we'd lost you." He suddenly puts his forehead between his hands on the steering wheel.

"Daddy?"

"I'm okay."

I leave my hand on his arm. After a moment he raises his head, puts his fingers under his sunglasses frame to wipe the tears away, then turns the key in the ignition. It makes a horrible grinding noise because he never turned off the engine. We look at each other and laugh.

. . .

The employee at the back gate of Macaw World takes one look at Teapot and her head snaps up. "That's a mallard."

"Yes." I say.

"Why would you rescue a mallard? The only thing worse is a Muscovy."

"Because I ran over it with an airboat, killed its brother, and scared its mother away."

The girl looks blankly at me.

I feel a moment of hopefulness. I'd be much happier taking Teapot back home. I glance at Dad.

"Young lady, I'm a . . . business associate of the owner, and we have his permission to bring this duckling here."

Dad dressed up to come here today. It's breaking my heart to see him pretending to be important for me and Teapot.

"But aside from that, you apparently don't know who my daughter is. She is the young woman who walked out of the Everglades, and this is the duckling she carried with her."

The girl's eyes widen. "That's Teapot?"

I nod.

"I'm sorry. That's like totally different." She holds the gate open for us. "My name's Amanda." She grins.

My insides roil with swallowed laughter. "Hello, Amanda. I'm Sarah."

Amanda leads us along the path past cages full of colorful parrots, many of which fly to the wire and chatter at us as we pass.

I leave the cardboard box in the car and carry Teapot in the folded-up hem of my T-shirt. My legs feel almost as heavy as they had trying to slog through calf-deep mud. Teapot trusts me to take care of her, to feed and protect her. She settles against my stomach and watches our progress with mild interest.

We reach the patio above a lawn that sweeps down to the pond where flamingos are feeding. A beautiful girl with auburn hair is sitting at a picnic table with a chimpanzee on her lap.

"She's deaf," Amanda says. "She and that chimp talk using sign language."

Both Dad and I smile at her. "What's the chimp doing here?" I ask.

"There's a rehab facility in the northwest corner." Amanda points off to her left. "That's Sukari. She was rescued from a laboratory somewhere."

There are ducks resting on the grass at the edge of the water. They are all mallards. One female has six newly hatched babies. It's amazing the difference two weeks have made. Teapot's more than three times their size.

When I put her on the grass, Teapot stretches, fluffs, flaps her wing nubs and shakes her pinfeather tail, then runs roly-poly toward the water. One of the male mallards gets up and charges Teapot, knocking her over.

I clap my hand over my mouth to keep from yelling at it.

Teapot rights herself and races up the incline with the male mallard, head low, right behind her. The adult duck draws up short when Teapot gets back to me and lodges herself between my ankles.

"They're not going to accept her," I tell Dad.

Amanda pulls on her chin like an old man with whiskers. "It may take some time. Let me go get some food and see if that distracts them."

I cuddle Teapot until Amanda returns. When she throws a fistful of cracked corn into the shallow water, all the ducks skid in and begin to dabble, some in water deep enough to upend. The mother duck and her babies stay on the edges of the frenzy, and it's toward them that I walk slowly with Teapot beside me. I position myself between the five adult ducks in the water and the mother and her babies, then scatter a handful of corn just off the end of my flip-flops. Teapot goes right to work and is quickly surrounded by babies. The mother duck waddles in, ignores Teapot, and begins to eat.

"This would be a good time to slip away," Amanda says. "If you'll call me tomorrow, I'll let you know how she's doing."

I feel Daddy put his arm around my shoulders, then the pressure of him turning me. As we walk slowly up toward the patio, I keep glancing back, waiting—wishing Teapot would look up and see me leaving.

Andy told me a python can go up to two years without food, but after a while, it will begin to feed on its own muscles. I wonder if it hurts like this when the snake begins to ingest its own heart. Tears run down my cheeks. "I feel so bad."

"I know, Honey." Daddy strokes my wild hair. "Love can sure knock the blocks out from under you."

I glance again at the deaf girl as we pass. Her expression is full of sympathy. She holds the chimpanzee so its head is pressed to her shoulder. "I know how you feel," she says.

I nod. "Thank you."

At the top of the hill, I look back. Teapot and the other babies are where the muddy, churned-up water laps at the shore. A sob catches in my throat. I turn and put my head against Dad's chest.

"Love lets go," he whispers.

I look back one last time. Teapot's sitting on the beach, preening. "I hope she forgets me quickly."

"I doubt that she will, but I don't think she'll mind much. She's safe here."

"I guess."

We start back past the cages of parrots.

"You know what helped me keep going, out there?"

He shakes his head.

"Remembering how we used to hang out together. Why don't we ever fish anymore, or dig turtle nests?"

Daddy shrugs. "I thought you'd outgrown doing those things with your old dad."

"Maybe I did for a while, but in the Everglades, I kept remembering those times and I realized how much I missed them." I take his hand.

EPILOGUE

Amanda from Macaw World called today. Teapot's fine.

I wait another week, then ride my bike there to see for myself. Amanda lets me in the back gate and then leaves me to sit alone at one of the picnic tables. If Teapot wasn't the odd-sized duck, I wouldn't have recognized her. She's doubled in size again.

All the ducks are used to people, so none look up when I sit down. Teapot is a little apart from the mother duck and her babies, but she's clearly become part of that family. I try to will her to look at me.

The flamingos are feeding, walking in a group of about twenty, all with their heads upside down, bills sweeping from side to side. A little boy runs by me and down the hill toward the ducks. His arms are spread like he's trying to take off. I jump up protectively, but Teapot and the others waddle unalarmed into the water and drift just out of reach. It's when I'm standing on the hill that Teapot looks directly at me, and there is a moment of recognition, like I'm someone from her past she can't quite place. I get that a lot. People have seen my picture in the paper but think they actually know me. Teapot is still watching me when the little boy's mother heads down to fetch him.

"Stay out of the mud," she says.

He laughs and begins to stomp up and down just at the water's edge, elbows flared.

The mother duck leads her babies into deeper water. Teapot turns and follows them.

. . .

Maybe there's a patron saint that takes care of lost causes, but all the things that were wrong at school aren't anymore. I made friends with a girl who's on the swimming team with me, and the AABCs—Amanda, Amanda, Brittany, and Courtney—act like we were friends before I became the school celebrity. But the best change is in Andy's father. This month, when he came to Miami to see his parole officer, he brought Andy with him. We didn't do much, just wandered in and out of the shops at CocoWalk and went to see a movie where we held hands, and when we were walking back to where we were supposed to meet his dad, he put his arm around my shoulders.

"Dad got a job."

"That's great, Andy." I love the weight of his arm.

"One of his buddies is fighting cancer, so Dad leased his boat for the stone crab season. I'm helping him on weekends. Maybe you'd like to come out with us one day."

"I doubt your dad would go for that."

"I ripped that flag down, Sarah, and he never said a word."

"He didn't?"

"Nope. I think he figured out what a jerk he was and is trying to change."

"Well, I hope he makes it."

"I'll be sixteen in a couple of months, you know. Then I can drive myself over."

"We'd better not tell my parents. They may not want me dating an older man."

Andy looks at me, then grins when he realizes I'm kidding.

. . .

Teapot turned out to be a boy.

ACKNOWLEDGMENTS

I was a pitifully poor student in school, partly because of some vision problems, but mostly because I hated certain subjects, like English and foreign languages, but loved others, like science and math. History and social studies were okay, but it says something that I remember the names of only two of my middle-school teachers, both of whom were—in my memory—fantastic. One was Ms. Andrews, my eighth-grade algebra teacher, and the other was Mr. Vickers, my seventh-grade science teacher. It may not be too much of an exaggeration to say they saved me from completely abandoning my education. While I accomplished only Cs and Ds in other subjects, I made As in math and science. The importance of those As would influence the course of my life from then on. No matter how poorly I did in middle school and later in high school, I knew I had the ability to do better. In other words, I wasn't lacking the intelligence; I was lacking the maturity to tackle subjects I didn't like. That's a very important distinction.

As mere coincidence, Mr. Vickers was on one of my flights some years later when I was a flight attendant for National Airlines. I didn't tell him what I just told you. I didn't know it then. I hadn't gone back to school yet. That didn't happen until 1977, when I enrolled in University of Miami, so I didn't know enough to thank him. For years, I wished I had. I wish I'd told him then that he was a wonderful teacher. I wished this so much that a few months ago I called my middle school to see if anyone there remembered him. By that afternoon, I was in contact with his daughter and his son-in-law, and by the next day in touch with him. I finally got to say thank you. It felt wonderful.

I also wish to thank the members of my writing groups: Norma Watkins, Katherine Brown, Maureen Eppstein, Katy Pye, and Jeannie Stickle. They are the most recent of my helpmates. There were dozens of classmates in graduate school who also had a hand in shaping this story as far back as I can remember. In fact, I've been noodling it for years, first as the true account of my husband's experiences walking out of the Everglades, then in the fictional form it now takes. The first person to critique this was Nobel Prize–winning author Isaac Bashevis Singer, who taught with Lester Goren at UM in the early 1980s. "Dis is real writing," he said. So, like Sarah and Andy, I slogged on.

Thanks also to Suzanne Byerley's editing skills, and Ralph Bellman, who knows the 'Glades like the back of his hand, and Teresa Sholars, who traveled to Florida with me when I was finishing up my research and got her feet wet.

Thanks always to Laura Dail, my fabulous agent, and to Andrew Karre, an editor worth his salt.